Twin Tales

KIERA COLSON

Published by Author Academy Elite
PO Box 43, Powell, OH 43065
www.AuthorAcademyElite.com

Identifiers:
LCCN: 2020913724
ISBN: 978-1-64746-397-7 (paperback)
ISBN: 978-1-64746-398-4 (hardback)
ISBN: 978-1-64746-399-1 (ebook)

Available in paperback, hardback, e-book, and audiobook

Dedication

To my family who stuck with me through every obstacle and to one of my best friends, Haylin Ownby, who has been with me since the very first rough draft.—K.C.

Table of Contents

Chapter 1: Legends Confirmed 1

Chapter 2: New Legs Upon Dry Sand 9

Chapter 3: Queen Ramona's Quarters 13

Chapter 4: Adopted 19

Chapter 5: Separate Lives 26

Chapter 6: Captain Who? 36

Chapter 7: A Terrible Fate 43

Chapter 8: Becoming a Pirate 46

Chapter 9: Swords and More 50

Chapter 10: Bon Voyage 57

Chapter 11: One's Loss Is Another's Gain 65

Chapter 12: Banished and Abandoned 74

Chapter 13: Tears of Crystal. 86

Chapter 14: Land. 92

Chapter 15: A Magical Encounter. 102

Chapter 16: Merena. 109

Chapter 17: Alone No More. 117

Chapter 18: Diamonds, Jewels, and More 120

Chapter 19: An Uncertain Future. 124

Chapter 20: Prisoner 132

Chapter 21: Scars of the Past, Present, and Future. . . . 137

Chapter 22: An Unexpected Ally 146

Chapter 23: Family History 156

Chapter 24: The Power of Magic Within. 164

Chapter 25: One Touch 170

Chapter 26: An Old Friend 179

Chapter 27: The King. 188

Chapter 28: An Army Like Never Before. 194

Chapter 29: The Trident and the Sceptre. 199

Chapter 30: Broken Shells Restored 203

Epilogue 207

About the Author 209

CHAPTER ONE

Legends Confirmed

*O*nce upon a time...
Merena, a young mother, sat upon a rock that peeked out over the ocean. As her sapphire blue tail rested upon the great rock, she stared at the sun as it sank just beyond the horizon. A gust of wind blew her long, wavy, jet-black hair out of her face. The wind subsided into a breeze as it brushed against her newborn twins' faces. Holding her treasures close, she captured the picture before her. She had never seen the sky painted as beautiful as it was that night. Her life had not been perfect, but she cherished moments like these—magical times when there was no storm, and the waves were at peace, when a smile takes the place of the cherished cries produced by her twins, and when it seemed a hidden artist had painted a masterpiece just for her. These moments never lasted long enough, but they were everlasting in her heart.

As the sun sank, the darkness stepped into its position of rulership. The waves became uneasy as they splashed against the rock where Merena rested. Holding her mergirls tight, she glanced around as the sea began to convulse. This unrest pushed her into confusion; she had not sensed a storm. She tried to comfort herself with thoughts of reason. Maybe she was just nervous because she would soon take on the responsibility of the entire merkingdom. With her heart pounding against her chest, she took one last glance into the darkness before diving into the deep blue sea.

As the water hit her face, a queasy feeling filled her once peaceful heart. Merena ached at the sound of her merbabies' cries as the water flowed past their fragile faces.

An instant later, a pain shot through her tail. Gasping for air, she launched forward in an attempt to stop the pain, but it relented not. Something was attached to her tail, and it was tightening every second. At the same time, the seafloor was becoming more distant with each unfolding moment. Fear struck her as she held even tighter to her children. *Was it the monsters from her childhood stories? Had she been captured by the feared enemy that lurked above the sea?*

With blurry vision, Merena glanced back one last time at her home beneath the sea, realizing that all of the terrible stories were true. The land creatures had captured her! Her first instinct was to save her daughters. She would not let her daughters' lives be demolished by those monsters. So, as her tail was about to break the water's surface, reluctantly, she let go of her two treasures, her "twin tales" as she called them. Her heart ached as the objects of her love faded from sight. At the same time, she lost grip of the dream she had for their lives; limp, numb, and desperately hoping this was all a horrible nightmare from which she would awake. Unfortunately, she knew this would not be so as she crashed through the surface of the deep blue sea.

A nauseating smell filled her nose as her head jerked out of the water. Struggling to discover what was happening, she flopped like a fish on dry ground. Merena's eyes widened as she saw that a giant hook was attached to her tail. That would explain the numb feeling that had begun to creep up her body. As she dangled in mid-air, she tried to turn herself around so she could see who . . . or what had done this to her. It was useless. Pain overwhelmed every part of her being. She had no strength left.

"I can't believe it. That's three this month," a low-pitched voice said from somewhere behind Merena. This sound triggered fear in Merena like no other. The legend of earth monsters had become real. *Was she about to become just another warning story merparents told their children?*

A demanding high-pitched voice jolted Merena back to reality, "Well? What is it? A shark? A squid? An octopus? It had better be something worth millions because you just interrupted my beauty sleep."

"Yes, ma'am," A masculine voice fearfully replied, "Yes, I pr-pr-promise," he stuttered.

"Is that what I think it is?" The demanding voice perked up. "Or Is this some kind of joke?"

"No, ma'am. James and I would never joke with you."

"Bring it in closer. I wanna see it," the high-pitched demanded. "Now, James!!"

Merena could hear someone running, and then all of a sudden, her pain intensified as her body swung to the left. A sinking feeling filled her stomach as she watched the water move beneath her.

Closing her eyes, Merena prayed a silent whisper, *God, no matter what shall happen to me, send someone kind and motherly to my daughters.*

With a thump, her body landed on something hard. Opening her eyes, Merena saw that she was on the surface of the creatures' vessel. With all her strength, Merena tried to find the monster that owned the voice she had just heard,

3

but it was still no use. Weak and dehydrated, Merena laid her head down in defeat.

"Wow, she's gorgeous." A short creature with dark red hair grinned down at Merena. His skin was red as fire and felt rough as it touched Merena's face. *Is this the creature the legends described as a man?* The creature did not have terrifying fangs or wings of fire like the legends of her past had proposed. He looked rather harmless with two twigs below his torso instead of a tail. Merena flinched as he lifted her head and examined it like she was for sale. Another man that looked similar to the first walked into Merena's line of vision. He looked exactly like the man next to him. *Was she seeing double?*

"How much do you think she's worth, James?" the one on the left exclaimed as if he was looking at a hidden treasure. Wishing she could move and slap the two ignoramuses before her, Merena tried to lift her arm, but pain overtook her effort.

"Oh, she's alive!" the demanding voice spoke up once again from somewhere behind Merena. *Clip. Clop. Clip. Clop.* Chills raced down Merena's spine as the footsteps of the creature came closer. *Clip. Clop. Clip. Clop.* The sound stopped. Merena lifted her head to see that the two duplicate creatures had now stepped back, and the real monster replaced them, a towering creature with blond hair pulled back into a tight bun. A large purple and black gown nearly swallowed her whole. Thorns ran up the heels of her shoes, under her dress, and all the way up to the crown that laid upon her head.

"Are you scared, fish? Well, don't be. I won't kill you." The woman leaned down exposing her extremely large chest compared to the creatures behind her. Her pointy nails scraped against Merena's face as the creature pushed a stray piece of Merena's hair back in place, "In fact, I have a present for you. Jaxon and James, go retrieve the gift."

"Yes ma'am," the two said in unison.

The monster shined its pearly white teeth at Merena. "I think we are going to get along just fine. You are going to be staying with me for a little while." Merena dreaded every sound released from the creature's mouth. She wanted to speak and ask questions, but she couldn't even lift her head. Merena knew it was because of the pain but also feared it was because she had never been out of the ocean this long before.

"Here you are, your majesty. You are a magnificent woman," James handed her a mysterious conch-shell. *So this is a woman? She definitely did not appear to breathe fire like the legends had foretold, but then again, the dangerous look in the woman's eye threatened otherwise.*

The woman grabbed Merena's hand and placed the large shell into it. All of a sudden, Merena's body stiffened into paralyzation. Her hand began to shake out of control. Struggling to release the shell from her uncontrollable grasp, Merena let out a scream of pain. Pain shot down her arm as the shell began to shrink. Pulling on it with her free hand, she struggled uselessly to remove it.

"Please make it stop!" Merena screamed. The pain was unbearable, piercing through her whole body now. She could feel her heartbeat in rhythm with the pain. Then it stopped. Dropping her hand to the ground, she opened her eyes to see that the shell had vanished. Looking up in confusion, Merena searched for any explanation of the pain she had just experienced.

The mysterious woman squatted down and grabbed her hand. She forced it open revealing a conch-shell marking upon Merena's palm. Frozen, Merena stared at what the shell had become. The woman began pressing down on the marking, causing it to glow.

Grinning, the mysterious woman whispered into Merena's ear, "Dear, sweet girl, your life is now mine. As long as you have the mark of my kingdom branded upon your skin, you belong to me!" Pain shot up Merena's tail once more as the hook ripped out her scales.

Merena felt herself rising again, but this time she could see nothing except a bright light. Confused, she struggled to catch sight of what was happening to her. A brutal pain filled every part of her body, leaving her wishing she had the strength to scream. The light faded back into darkness, and she fell back upon the vessel with a thud. Opening her eyes, Merena started to focus. All of the pain had subsided. As realization kicked in, she saw before her a pair of legs. She looked around, praying that they weren't hers and that she still had her gorgeous tail. But the stories were true; her gorgeous tail was gone, replaced with a pair of legs in blue jean shorts. All that was left was the locket that her mother and father had given her when she was born, nestled on top of the dark blue tank top that now covered her torso.

"Welcome to our world, fish. Now that you don't have a hook in your fin and you aren't in pain, is there anything you would like to say?" the woman asked.

So many questions filled Merena's mind, but she couldn't seem to form words to speak.

"Well then, I guess I will speak first." The woman pointed at the two men beside her, "This is Jaxon and James. You will do whatever they say because they do whatever I say." She paused, "Oh, and you must be wondering what has happened to your ugly tail."

In total shock, Merena nodded. None of the stories she was told as a kid had consisted of this type of magic.

"You see, darling, I took it. But don't worry. If you serve me well, it may be possible for you to win your tail back," she said, with an eerie smile. "And there are many others like you that work for me. You'll do just fine. Now tell me. What is your name?" An evil smirk crossed her face.

Merena looked at her new legs before trying to speak. At first, nothing came out, but she was finally able to say three shaky words, "I am Merena."

"She speaks," laughed James and Jaxon.

"Well, Merena," The woman paused. "I am Queen Ramona of Hysteria, and you, my dear, are now under my control. James, Jaxon, take her to the cell and get this boat back to the mainland. I must continue my beauty sleep."

"Queen Ramona?" Jaxon asked with a pitch of fear, "Why did you turn her into a human? Don't you have enough of them? Couldn't we have become rich with the reward money?"

"Jaxon, I am the Queen. Why do you think the law requires to return these fish to me? I have all the money in the world. You shall never question my ways again, or I will turn you into a fish and eat you for dinner!" screamed Queen Ramona as she stormed off towards the captain's quarters.

Unsure of what had just taken place, Merena tried to move her legs. Without warning, James and Jaxon pulled her to her feet.

"Listen, fish, we've done this many times. Just go left foot, right foot, left foot, right foot." Jaxon demonstrated. Merena tried, but the ground seemed to be swaying. Each time she moved one of her legs, it was if she was lifting a thousand-pound weight.

After what felt like a mile, they arrived at a square door on the floor. Jaxon opened it, and before Merena could say a word, James threw her in. Merena tumbled into a deep, dark blackness, hitting the ground once again with a thud. Darkness invaded her sight. The ground beneath her rolled back and forth.

James locked the door as he looked down at her. "She's gotta be the prettiest mermaid we've ever caught."

Laying her head down, Merena touched her new, unwanted legs for the first time. They were soft and fragile, unlike her tough, massive, and powerful tail. She rubbed at the marking on her skin that had brought this burden upon her, but it only sent another striking pain down her spine. Hopeless, she closed her eyes. An emptiness ate at her as she remembered how full her arms had been only a few hours before. Merena knew she would never forget the peace that had come with embracing her daughters. Whispering a prayer that they were safe, she sent her love to them … wherever they may be. She closed her eyes and struggled off to sleep.

CHAPTER TWO

New Legs Upon Dry Sand

"Get up!" A loud voice awoke Merena without warning. Desperately praying it had all been a bad dream, she searched for her highly decorated tail. When her eyes saw the truth, her heart sank like a rock in the ocean.

"Get up!" Looking up she saw the two men who had captured her. She put forth great effort to stand but she still didn't understand how this leg thing worked.

One of the men above let out a yawn as he opened the door and started to climb down into the cage. Merena flinched as he grabbed her arm and tossed her on his back. Merena pushed against the man's grasp, but it was no use. She had been trained to fight megalodons and giant octopuses, but it was all with her magnificent tail. Weak and untrained in this new world, Merena watched herself yet again rise in the air as one of the twins carried her up to the top deck.

The two men left her standing there alone. Her glance followed a bird as it flew free out into the great ocean. The bird changed directions, flying in a great circle. A gasp escaped Merena's mouth as her eyes saw what was before her—great, elevated mountains filled the landscape. Hundreds of birds of many colors soared in and out of their mountainous home. Never had she been so close to the forbidden world. As horrifying as the creatures that ruled it were, Merena could not deny how beautiful the landscape was.

Gazing to see where Jaxon and James had wandered off to, Merena saw Queen Ramona looking down on her from the top deck. Quickly looking away, Merena saw James and Jaxon laying out a really long board that led to the sand below. Taking baby steps, Merena made her way towards the railing of the ship. She looked down at the beach, scanning for other creatures like herself. She saw none. In fact, she didn't see a single animal of any type on the beach floor. Merena had read that the creatures above would spend all day on the beach searching for the homes of crabs, stealing them away for their own pleasure.

"Where are the rest of you?" Merena called out to Jaxon who had already stepped foot onto the sand.

"The rest of the humans?" he questioned.

Merena nodded her head as James returned the answer, "This is a private beach. Only Queen Ramona and her highly valued servants touch this sand."

"Speaking of touching the sand, James. Get the gorgeous little lady and take her down there. We need to start heading home," Queen Ramona's voice rang out loud and clear. Turning around to see, Merena was startled to find Queen Ramona standing inches away from her face. Her breath smelt of seaweed and rotten fish. It was all Merena could do to keep from squinching her face in disgust.

James spun Merena back around and dragged her across the deck and down the ramp. Merena nearly jumped fifty feet in the air the moment her bare feet touched the burning sand. It was rough, sticky, unpleasant, and nothing like the sand beneath the sea. She tried walking again, but this time it was harder than ever. Her skin felt as if she was walking on fire. With each biting step, the sand seemed to move beneath her. Taking a deep breath, Merena took a large step forward only to be launched face-first into the sea of sand before her. Outbursts of laughter from Queen Ramona and the twins filled her ears. James pulled Merena up, nearly tossing her back into the sand due to all his laughter. Eyes burning, Merena spit out the gritty sand from her mouth and let James lead the way, hoping they weren't walking much farther in the burning sand.

James snarled, "Remember, it's right, left, right, left."

James and Jaxson directed her towards the side of a rocky mountain. They stopped and glanced back. *Probably looking for Queen Ramona or a tourist,* Merena thought. Sand hit the back of Merena's legs causing her to jump in startlement.

Queen Ramona stepped beside her and laughed, "Are you afraid of sand? Don't you have sand where you are from? Never mind…Now, let's get a move on."

Suddenly Merena noticed that there was another woman standing next to Queen Ramona. She was tall with gorgeous brown hair. Her light blue eyes seemed to enhance her beauty greatly. The woman seemed to be in a different world as she stared at the crashing waves behind them. Her gaze slowly fell upon Merena. A chill raced down Merena's spine as she wondered if the girl had any emotions at all, for her face was a blank canvas. Merena fearfully wondered if she was about to enter the world that had erased this poor girl's smile.

As Queen Ramona walked toward the rock wall, the woman held Queen Ramona's dress so it would not touch the ground. Before Merena could ask the mysterious woman's name, Queen Ramona pushed a rock back. The sand shifted beneath Merena's feet as a larger portion of the mountain wall slid open, revealing only darkness. James went first, then Queen Ramona, and next, the mystery woman.

"Let's go, little fishy," Jaxson pushed Merena towards the opening. With every step Merena knew her glorious life was slipping away. *No more musical performances with her dolphin friends or full moon dates with the love of her life.* Walking deeper into the darkness, Merena felt a heavy hopelessness fall upon her. She did not want to become like the beautiful girl that walked inches in front of her. She wanted to be free like the birds that flew in the sky. Glancing back at the rock door closing behind her, Merena promised herself to never lose hope of seeing her daughters once again.

❧

Midnight

Later that night, a sharp pain tossed Merena out of the make-shift bed Queen Ramona had prepared for her. Grabbing her side, Merena nearly screamed as dark blue blood began to gush from her. An eerie glow emitted from within her. The blood stopped, slowing and thickening nearly as fast as it had begun. Heart racing, Merena felt a heaviness fill her heart. Her body rolled over in agony, gasping for air. Rolling her shirt up, Merena felt her body nearly go limp at what she saw. Two nearly identical scars that stretched from her ribs to her hip. The scars were the shape of a crown with three points. Merena knew that this type of scar could only come from the Sapphire Trident, her father's trident. Rolling her shirt back down, Merena threw herself upon her pillow and began to wail. *This couldn't be happening. They couldn't be gone.* The mark of the trident only appears on the rightful ruler of the Northern Merkingdom each time someone is unrightfully killed by it. And the two marks up her skin, Merena feared, were the marks of a king and queen.

CHAPTER THREE

Queen Ramona's Quarters

Merena folded the sheets on her bed for the fourteenth time since she'd been in Queen Ramona's castle. Twenty beds were lined up against the walls of her room. There were ten on each side with one girl per bed. Each servant had one-night stand for the few things they had. There had to be at least ten other rooms like this one. Filled with women, just like Merena, all throughout Queen Ramona's castle. A set of chores were given to each servant each day. Their jobs would last from sunrise to sunset.

Each servant was dressed in a different colored dress that puffed at the sleeves. It was completed with a white apron in front, mob-cap upon their heads, and a pair of dark colored flats. Most of Queen Ramona's servants had a dark red, a dull yellow, or an ugly green dress. Merena assumed it showed where they were from because hers was the only dress that was a deep ocean blue, the same as her tail once was.

Walking towards the door of the bedroom, Merena saw lonely faces all around her. Each girl longed to talk, but a fear of what Queen Ramona would do if they were caught controlled them.

The past two weeks had been the longest and hardest days in Merena's pampered life. Although Merena loved her previous life and it did have its emotional downfalls, she wished she had had a more physically difficult life. It would have prepared her for the servanthood she was now under. She worked endlessly with only five hours of sleep each night. Merena grabbed her chore list for the day out of the long bin near the door. She sighed. The card she had been given explained that she had to serve Queen Ramona personally for the day. She had yet to receive this assignment but had heard that it was dreadful.

Ding! Ding! The breakfast bell filled Merena's ears as she picked up her pass and headed towards the dining hall.

The Dining Room was the same size as all the bedrooms, except that there was an extremely long table with non-matching chairs around it. Hurrying to get in line for breakfast, Merena wondered if perhaps today they would have something different. Since she had gotten here it had been the same thing for breakfast, lunch, and dinner. She picked up her tray and held it out for the large, bald man who served them each morning.

"What are we having today?" Merena asked like she did each morning.

Plop! "Squid Pudding," the man said with a smile.

Merena looked at the squishy mess on her plate, "Same as yesterday."

"Keep a-movin'," the man nodded her on down the line. Her stomach ached. It longed for something nutritious.

Merena sat near the door of the room in case she needed to get up in a hurry. She played with the food on her plate as

14

she watched everyone else gobble it up. *I guess they all have gotten used to eating what used-to-be their friends.*

"Hey, are you going to eat your breakfast?" a young girl across from her asked, "or are you just going to stare at us?"

This was the first person to talk to Merena since she had arrived, "I am not that hungry. Would you like it?"

The girl grabbed her plate and ate it right up.

"Did you used to have a squid friend?" the girl asked, mouth still full.

Merena nodded. Jess was the funniest sea creature alive. If you needed a laugh he somehow was always near. He'd come flying in to save the day but then crash into something. A smile escaped her face as she got lost in her memories.

"We all understand. We are just like you, ya know," the girl touched Merena's hand. There was a marking upon the girl's skin that matched Merena's perfectly, "But once you get hungry enough, you don't care what you eat. Well, I gotta go. Time to get started on my chores."

Merena started to ask for her name, but she was gone. Vanished in the sea of lost girls.

Putting her tray up, Merena made her way towards the servant entrance of the main castle. Merena had often wondered if the rest of the castle was as dull as the walls down here. Today was destined to be different, because even though she was to serve the Queen, at least she could feed her curiosity. She had not seen the light of day since she had entered the cave. Not knowing whether there would be windows in the upper castle, Merena longed to feel the warm sun against her skin.

With all her strength, she pulled open the stone door. *Maybe I should have eaten my breakfast.* Merena could feel how weak she had become since she had been captured.

Merena proceeded cautiously as she went up a steep staircase. At the top, there was another door, but this time she pushed. A great light stung Merena's eyes as the door flung open. Stepping into the unknown, Merena watched in awe as the beauty of the castle unfolded before her eyes. In front of her was a one-hundred-foot ceiling with curtains that flowed from the ceiling to the floor. Everything was either black, purple, or silver. Great thorns wrapped around the walls. Some even touched the couches in the living room.

"Hey, Merena! It's me, James!" his voice shocked Merena.

Merena nodded as he continued speaking, "Come, come. You've got lots to do today." Grabbing her shoulder, James directed Merena down a great hallway. Servants were coming in and out of the halls.

Merena felt strange. None of the girls here would make eye contact with her, or anyone for that matter. They just kept their heads down and worked.

After passing multiple rooms they came to a giant door with thorns that spiraled up each side of it. James stepped back and nodded Merena forward. Grabbing the ice-cold knob, Merena slowly turned it.

No light was shining through this room. It was dark and purple, extremely purple. This room had to be Queen Ramona's bedroom. It seemed to be half a football field long with a massive bed at the end of the room. Taking another step in, Merena glanced around for Queen Ramona but did not see her.

"I am right here, darling," her voice cracked the silence of the room. A dark shadow turned towards Merena from the right corner of the room. Today, Queen Ramona was wearing a long black cap with a purple pantsuit. Her hair was half up, half down with thorns throughout it.

"I'm glad you could join me. Come sit," she motioned towards chairs that had been placed in front of an unlit fireplace. Merena followed behind Queen Ramona and waited for her *awful* Majesty to sit.

Clap! Clap! The fireplace exploded into blue flames. Amazed, Merena wondered how it was even possible. All her readings about the world above had told of great dangerous red fires, not blue seemingly controlled ones.

16

"You must be wondering why I chose you to serve me today," Queen Ramona took back Merena's attention. Shaking slightly, Merena nodded.

Queen Ramona's eyes scanned Merena, "I've had my servants watch you. You're different from the other girls around you. You have a glow in your eyes that's different. You have what we humans call stupid, but you sea creatures call hope. Why?" Unsure how to answer, Merena looked towards the ground as if she'd find answers there.

"Answer me, fish," Queen Ramona was becoming uneasily impatient.

"Queen Ramona, I am different because, as you said, I do have hope," Merena struggled to think of something else to say,

"But why? Who are you?" Queen Ramona questioned.

Merena, without thinking, told the truth, "I am Princess Merena of the Northern Sea Kingdom."

"You're a princess! But aren't you supposed to have powers?" Queen Ramona shifted in her seat.

A deep sorrow filled Merena's heart, "No. I did not receive my power before you captured me. I am a late bloomer, I suppose."

"Oh, really," Queen Ramona said with fake pity, "Tell me about your family?"

"They are my hopes and dreams. I have twin daughters, and.... ," Merena felt her heart drop.

"So, it was only you and your daughters? No one else?" Queen Ramona seemed to be filled with joy.

"No. I had a family, a husband. On the day you captured me, however, I wanted to spend some time alone with my daughters before I became extremely busier. I was to become queen soon," a great longing continued to fill Merena's soul.

Queen Ramona seemed like she was about to burst, "Where are your children now? And your kingdom, what will happen to it?"

"My daughters are lost to the waves, but I have faith they will find their way home. And my merkingdom? We have suffered great loss before. We are strong and will thrive again," Merena straightened up.

"You seem very sure of yourself," Queen Ramona laughed, "Thank you for speaking with me. You may begin your day by making my bed," Merena stood up and walked toward the bed.

"Merena, I just thought of something wonderful. You don't deserve to be with all of the other servants, because … like you said, you're *royalty*. You are different and you must be separated from the others in order to stay that way. I don't want you to lose any *hope*. So, I'd like you to be my personal servant, *forever*. You will stay in the room next to mine and be with me at all times," she paused, "Oh, I intend on finding those daughters of yours. That way the whole royal family can live Happily Ever After … in the palms of my hands." An evil smile possessed Queen Ramona as she looked out the sole window in her room.

A terrible feeling rushed through Merena. Her dreams had been taken away, but she promised herself that she would never let this sea-witch take away her daughters' dreams as well.

CHAPTER FOUR

Adopted

Merena's newborn twins rested at the bottom of the ocean floor, their fate left to the unknown. The sea became unsteady as a school of fish swam by causing the twins to float apart. A pod of dolphins chased after the school of fish. One of the dolphins trailed behind the pod to look at a coral community. Taking in the vibrant colors of the mini world around him, the dolphin's eyes connected with one of the twins. Confused, the dolphin touched the infant merchild. A smile crossed the baby's face as it reached up at the dolphin. The dolphin looked at the jewel before him. The baby mergirl had long jet-black hair with eyes that reminded him of a bright, full moon. Her tail was a beautiful light blue that blended into a deep, dark, sea blue. Warmth and peace filled the dolphin's heart. *How could he just leave it here? It would surely die.* Scooping the merchild up, he let out a sound of joy as he swam away towards his pod.

Sand swept over the lost infant that lay within a massive seaweed bed. Scared of the dark and lonely, the merbaby began to cry. A dark shadow moved above the merchild. The cries of the merbaby increased, filling the waters. The shadow came closer, revealing a beautiful young mermaid. She wore an orange top that brought out the bright yellow in her tail. Her brown eyes complimented her blond hair that flowed down her back.

"Who are you?" the young mermaid questioned. Picking up the merchild, she wondered how it had been left here.

"Hush now, everything is going to be alright," she said as she rocked the infant. Swimming out of the seaweed bed, the mermaid looked around for the mother of the merbaby. All she saw was a pod of dolphins swimming towards the Eastern Sea Kingdom. She glanced upon the merchild's dark, black hair that gracefully moved with the water. Her eyes were a crystal blue that shimmered ever so slightly. Her tail was a dark blue that faded into a lighter blue.

Looking upon her discovery, the young mermaid smiled, "Don't worry, little one. I'll keep you safe. You can live with my family." Excited to tell her family about the darling baby mergirl she had found, the mermaid swam towards the Western Sea Kingdom as fast as her tail could go.

※

The dolphin pod made their way into a massive cave that they proudly called home. The dolphin laid the baby mergirl on an old oyster shell that had been used for a baby dolphin bed the year before. The dolphins had traveled to the outer parts of the Eastern Sea Kingdom, the main home of whales, dolphins, and porpoises.

Curious about the mermaid before them, the dolphins surrounded her. Never had they seen a mermaid that contained such dark hair and crystal eyes. One of the younger dolphins touched its nose on the baby mergirl. The mergirl burst into laughter, sending the young dolphin back with fright. A mother dolphin nudged the young dolphin towards the mergirl, reassuring her that everything was alright. The young dolphin rested its nose on the mergirl and smiled as the merbaby reached towards the top of the dolphin's nose.

Leaving the young dolphin with the merchild, the elder dolphins floated to the council room of the cave. Forming a circle, each dolphin whispered in its own anticipation, each unsure of what they would do with the infant.

Translation:

"What are we supposed to do with this merchild?" the dolphin nearest to the door questioned.

"I propose we keep her. She is just a baby and it would be wonderful to raise a merchild," the dolphin that had found the mergirl commented.

"No, she is not one of us. How do you expect us to raise a different creature of the sea?" questioned another.

"And plus, she would grow up learning the dolphin tongue, instead of her native one," one dolphin chimed in.

"I will teach her both," the dolphin that had found her assured.

"But who knows what would happen if the Eastern Sea Mermaids found her. She looks nothing like them," a soft voice added.

The dolphins continued to express their opinions, all at once, each fearful of what would happen if they either kept or gave away the mergirl.

"Silence!" a stern voice from the back of the cave commanded.

The eldest and wisest dolphin swam to the center of the circle as the rest of the dolphins became as silent as a preying shark.

Looking around, the eldest dolphin continued, "This precious treasure has been given to us to protect and serve. I believe it is our duty to raise her. We found her for a reason, and we will do everything in our ability to bring her up in a loving and caring home. We will not burden her upon someone else. Is that clear?"

The dolphins all nodded and watched her swim over to the merchild.

Picking up the mergirl, the dolphin smiled, "Welcome to the family, Evalyn."

Swimming as fast as she could the young mermaid made her way towards the Western Sea Kingdom, known for their vast variety of seashells. Entering the gates of her merkingdom, the mermaid made her way through the crowd of merfolk. Brilliant oranges and yellows made her feel at home as she turned down the lively street where she lived. Her home was just like the other shell homes in the city. It was two stories high with shell bricks all over the front. Some of the more expensive homes had giant Lucine Shells as the front of their homes and others even had Cerith Shells that spiraled up towards the surface of the sea.

The mermaid loved the merkingdom where she was being raised. It was the brightest of the four merkingdoms that existed below the waves. It was nearest to the surface, but furthest away from the humans. The mermaids that lived there were considered the most artistic of all. The Western Sea Kingdom mermaids had yellow and orange tails that shimmered at any time of day.

The young mermaid arrived at home and opened the giant, shell door. The normal business of her family met her eyes. Her two sisters were swimming around arguing over who would wear the yellow, pearl top to summer school the next day. Ignoring her sisters, the mermaid searched for her mother. She did not want the merbaby to cry and spoil her big surprise.

Glancing into the kitchen, the mermaid saw that her mother had just finished speaking on the shell phone.

"Mother, may I speak with you?" the mermaid asked as she watched her mother pull her blond hair into a loose bun.

Glancing up, the mother smiled at her daughter, "Of course, come here."

Hesitant, the mergirl paused before entering the room with the merbaby, "Mother, I need to show you something."

A sudden nervousness swept over the young mermaid. *What if her mother didn't want to help the merbaby?* Unsure of what her mother would say, the mermaid took a deep breath. Swimming into the kitchen, the young mermaid held the now sleeping merchild up to her mother.

"Tiera, is that a merbaby?" shocked and confused, the mother swam out from behind the kitchen counter.

Nodding Tiera explained, "I was exploring the seaweed bed when I heard a cry. I found her all alone. I searched for her family, but they were nowhere to be found."

Tiera heard the voices of her sisters get louder. Her mother directed her into the pantry as she took the merchild into her arms. Tiera admired her mother's graceful rocking of the merbaby. It was a true act of motherly love.

"We can't tell anyone you found her. Did you notice how she is decorated with dark blue shells and pearls? And look how different her tail is compared to ours," the mother inquired.

Tiera nodded, "That's why it took me so long to find her. Her tail and hair blended into the deep sea colors."

"Yes. She has to be from the Northern Sea Kingdom. They are known for their deep blue color, like we are known for our sunny colors," the mother explained.

"Why do you think she was so close to our border? Aren't the merkingdoms in terms to not come near each other?" Tiera questioned.

Pausing for a brief second, Tiera's mother felt the soft hair of the merbaby, "The Northern Sea Kingdom has been struggling. They used to be the most powerful of the four merkingdoms. However, ever since the last war, our merkingdom has been on the rise. The Northern Sea Kingdom is not the safest at the moment... They are in a rebuilding stage. That's why supposedly the King and Queen are handing the crown to their daughter."

Unsure of what her mother was going to do, Tiera let out the burning questions within her, "What will we do with the little mergirl?"

Sighing, Tiera's mother looked into the merbaby's eyes, "We can't take her back to the Northern Sea Kingdom, we'd be killed. However, it's against the law to protect someone from a foreign kingdom. We can't just toss the merchild back out to sea. And I know your father will never approve of us keeping her."

Deep in thought, Tiera looked into her mother's wise eyes. Even though Tiera wanted badly to keep the merchild, she knew her mother would make the best decision.

Tiera's mother confidently spoke, "I don't exactly know what we will do. However, I feel at peace with the decision that we need to keep her. Your sisters are going to Stingray College next month and it'll be you and me at home. Your father is always working and won't be home much, especially since his new promotion as an admiral. If your father asks anything about this, I will have to tell him, due to the respect and honor I have for him," looking straight into Tiera's eyes, "You cannot tell a single soul that we are raising this merchild. Our whole family would be banished, and our reputation ruined. It would be an absolute disgrace. But I know that I can trust you. I want you to understand that I am doing this because I feel that it is what we are being called to do."

Bursting with joy, Tiera wrapped her arms around her mother and the merbaby, "I promise to be the best big sister in the whole world."

"Tiera, you understand that you will have to come straight home after school. No clubs or sports, including water polo. You will have to help me take care of this merchild. We will both be her mother. If this merchild fails, it will be our fault. I want to see her grow and be able to live freely as you have," Tiera's mother handed the sleeping merchild back to her.

"I have never seen any mermaid more beautiful than her mother," Tiera studied the dark blue in the mergirl's tail.

Nodding, her mother continued to make a plan, "Your secret room behind your shell bed will now be hers. Tomorrow we will go out and buy the needed supplies for the merchild. I will make a list tonight."

"Mother, what will we call her?" Tiera asked.

"Now, that's an important decision," her mother looked through the glass in the pantry door to see if her two eldest daughters were still having at it. They were.

Tiera got lost in thought for a moment.

Alana. . .Misty. . .Jessica. . .Lana. . .I got it!

"Her name shall be Adelia!" Tiera looked at her new baby mersister.

Smiling, her mother looked at their new treasure, "Hello, Adelia."

CHAPTER FIVE

Separate Lives

10 Years Later

"*Evalyn, where are you?*" said Evalyn's dolphin friend, Lola. A giggle escaped from behind a large coral reef. Lola quickly raced over to catch the wild ten-year-old. Evalyn loved playing hide and seek. As Lola quietly got closer to the reef, she could see black hair floating from behind a red coral.

Swoosh! "Here I am!" Evalyn swirled up towards the surface. Her hair was black as night with bangs that completed her face. Her blue tail had grown long and seemed to blend into the water. But what Lola loved most about her adopted friend was her eyes. They shimmered like crystal and were always full of hope. Chasing after Evalyn, Lola wrapped her fins around her.

"*It's time to go back home,*" Lola expressed.

Evalyn looked around for a second, "But what about my other friends? We are playing hide and seek, remember?"

"*Oh, yeah. Tell them you have to go. But be quick,*" Lola smiled.

"Game over guys! We can play again tomorrow," Evalyn hollered at the top of her lungs.

All at once the creatures of the sea came out of hiding. Stingrays, seahorses, eels, clownfish, starfish, and more all came out to hug young Evalyn.

"Bye! See you tomorrow!" the sea creatures said as they let her go.

Waving goodbye, Evalyn exclaimed, "I'm it tomorrow!"

"Did you have a good day at school?" Lola asked as she pulled Evalyn in tight.

Evalyn turned onto her back to look Lola in the face, "Oh, yes, we played seahorse tag, hide and go seek, and we rode on Mrs. Stings back again. It was so much fun. I bet all the other schools of sea creatures are jealous."

Smiling, Lola questioned, "What did you learn about today?"

Swimming faster in excitement, Evalyn continued, "Well, Mrs. Stings took us to look at baby Atlantic salmon. They are going to hatch sometime this week and we get to see it happen! I can't wait! We also learned how to carve seashells. And when we are all done, we get to decorate the coral reef where all my friends live!"

"That sounds like so much fun, Evalyn!" Lola guided her back into the dolphin cave, "We are going to make some music tonight! We all think it's time for you to choose the instrument you will be playing in our band."

Evalyn looked around the cave, all the dolphins in the pod were waiting anxiously for Evalyn to come home. They had laid out all the instruments Evalyn had been dreaming about playing in front of her. There were oyster drums, coral flutes, starfish shakers, and conch shell horns. Scanning the ground, Evalyn frowned. This was a huge decision. She would be playing this instrument for a very long time. A sparkle caught her eye near one of the conch shell horns. Evalyn swam closer, examining the fragile instrument. A small blue light omitted from a brown conch shell with bits of blues, blacks, and white highlights. Picking it up, Evalyn felt a sense of peace flow through her. This was the one.

Evalyn placed her lips on the hole and blew. Nothing came out. Disappointment sank in Evalyn. She thought she was going to make a pretty sound like everyone else.

"Don't worry young one, in time you will become the best conch shell player in the eastern hemisphere," said the eldest dolphin, *"It's time to begin your lessons. Come join the other five conch shell players in the pod."*

A giant smile exploded upon Evalyn's face as she swam to the far corner of the cave. This was going to be the best day of her life.

⊗

Adelia admired her conch shell collection on her wall. She had over twenty different ones of all sizes that Tiera had gotten for her. Her room was small, but Tiera and her mother had allowed her to decorate it with fluorescent, glowing corals. Her bed was narrow enough to fit perfectly in the far corner of her room. It wasn't the most ideal place to spend basically twenty-four hours each and every day, but she managed.

Each day, Adelia waited for Tiera to come home and teach her what she had learned at school. Some days Tiera would bring her books from the Clownfish Library. Adelia loved books about the world outside her room. Just reading words on a page made her feel closer to the world. She was fascinated by the idea of being allowed to explore it with her own hands instead of her mind.

Tiera's mother had to run some errands today, so Adelia was instructed to stay in her room. On most days she would come out into the house, try on Tiera's clothes, and help Tiera's mother cook.

Thump. A sound came from behind Adelia 's door. Quickly she crunched down into the far corner of her room. Adelia took a deep breath, steadying her pounding heart. She was not fearful of being caught, because her blue tail and dark hair caused her to blend into most surroundings. The shell door cracked open, revealing a mermaid's blond hair.

"Adelia, it's me," Tiera swam into the room.

Over the past ten years, both of them had grown up a lot. Tiera had transformed into a passionate, young mermaid. Her tail was fully developed, long and yellow, with little diamond designs hidden within it. Her hair was long and her eyes full of much more knowledge. She continued down the same path as her sisters by going to Stingray College. While she was top of her class, her sisters, however, barely made a B-. Still fighting over what to wear, Tiera's sisters started a struggling fashion business together.

Adelia had grown into quite an intelligent ten-year-old. She absorbed everything Tiera told her. Her long tail seemed to be changing into a deeper ocean blue color every passing day. Her hair was long and dark with little light blue highlights beginning to develop.

Tiera looked into Adelia 's wandering crystal blue eyes, "I think today is the day."

"The day for what, Tiera?" Adelia swam closer to hear every word that Tiera was about to say.

"It's time for the surprise that I've been waiting to show you. I just needed you to get a little older," Tiera moved Adelia 's bed revealing a hole in the ground.

Excitement rushed through little Adelia, "What's that doing there?"

"Follow me," Tiera disappeared into the hole.

Adelia followed behind Tiera, curious about what lay beyond the tunnel.

"Is mother ok with this?" Adelia questioned.

"Yes, we have been planning this for you since you were three years old. We both knew you wouldn't be able to enjoy life as I have. I know it must be pretty boring in your room,"

Tiera explained, "You see your room used to be an addon to mine. Mother let me have a little place where I could escape from the chaos my sisters cause." Adelia focused on a small light in the distance. *Where could they be going?*

"How'd you dig this and why isn't mother coming with us?" Adelia wondered.

"We dug a little each night while the others were sleeping. It was a mother-daughter bonding experience, if you know what I mean…. This tunnel goes right under the city!" Tiera slowed her speed as she spoke, "Mother didn't think it would be a good idea for us to both be gone at the same time…. Adelia, are you ready?"

"For what? For what?" Adelia swam faster trying to see what was up ahead.

"The ocean!" Tiera spun out of the opening and into the great blue sea. The tunnel led away from the Western Sea Kingdom and into great open waters, "You are safe to explore here, Adelia. You can find shells like the ones I've brought you. You can explore caves and seaweed beds. Just like I was doing when I discovered you!"

Adelia took in the surroundings. Blue as far as she could see. Schools of fish played in the distance and dolphins swam above her. She had never dreamed that the world was so big and vast. There were an endless number of places for her to explore.

"Now you must remember that you are never to swim near the gates of any kingdom. You will surely be killed. You also should not talk to any other mermaids. They could turn on you. You must be careful who you trust," Tiera sternly looked at Adelia, "Do you promise?"

Swimming out a little, Adelia turned towards Tiera, "I promise."

"Then let's explore!" taking Adelia's hand, Tiera guided her towards the ocean floor, "I know the perfect place to show you first."

Squick! Evalyn blew into her conch shell. A spark of joy ran through her bones as she let out her first sound. Yes, it was not a beautiful conch shell noise like the others were making, but at least it was a sound!

"Here, watch me," Grace, the youngest dolphin, exclaimed.

A beautiful noise was released from her shell. The notes went up and down the scale perfectly. Evalyn watched her lips and fins move to make the magnificent sound. As the dolphin held a final, perfectly pinched note, applause erupted.

"It's just three simple steps. One, you have to blow real hard. Two, move your lips at the same time as your fins... er hands. And, three, feel the song that's deep in your heart. Now try again. It will come to you," encouraged Grace.

Evalyn closed her eyes; she listened to the song deep within her. Lifting up her shell, she felt her lips connect to the instrument and then she blew. The sound that flowed from the shell was of sorrow and pain. It was not beautiful nor joyful, it was real and raw. A sound so unbelievable to the dolphins who were witnessing it. The music that flowed out of Evalyn surprised them. They had only known a joyful little mergirl, but this revealed a mergirl who was confused and longing for answers. The sound calmed the waters around them. Sea creatures a mile away stopped and listened to the cry the merchild played.

Releasing the conch shell from her lips, Evalyn looked around at the sad faces, confused she held her conch shell close to her heart, "Did I do something wrong?"

"No dear, you did something most merfolk work for all their life. You released a song that was composed by your heart," the eldest dolphin spoke.

31

"All I did was play," Evalyn explained, "Is that not what you asked me to do?"

"You have done much more. You play as if you have practiced for centuries. You've shown us your heart," Lulu continued, "Do you know what your song is about?"

Evalyn stumbled to find her words, "I… I love my home here. I love my friends, but sometimes … at night," Evalyn paused. A heavy sorrow filled her heart.

Eyes watering, she continued, "You guys are my family, but sometimes I feel as if I am missing a part of me. At times I feel sad or happy for someone or something else. I can't explain it. And sometimes my mind wanders away from here. It dreams of what my mother is like. It wonders if my father is brave. I want to know why they left me."

A tear-like substance ran down the mergirl's face. Dropping to the sand floor, her tears hardened into sea glass. To humans, it was something they treasured, but to a mermaid, it was her sorrow, joy, and anger. It felt as if a thousand-pound whale had sat on Evalyn's chest. She could barely breathe. The dolphins embraced the poor mergirl. They had never seen her so fragile before.

After it felt as if she had emptied her soul, Evalyn lifted her head, "Sorry I cried. I have never felt that way before," taking a deep breath, she smiled, "Can you teach me some of your songs?"

The dolphins slowly nodded in agreement. All of their hearts ached for their hurting little mergirl.

"Let's sing Coral Reef," a dolphin suggested.

The dolphins let out a cheerful noise, grabbing their instruments. Evalyn swam over to the conch shell section.

"Just follow my lead and you'll do great. Trust me, you're a natural," Grace exclaimed.

Evalyn smiled and held her shell towards the sky and waited for the conductor to give the signal to play. His fin seemed to move in slow motion as he signaled the conch shell section to play. As Evalyn blew into her newly found passion, she felt a calming peace flow through her. This was a new chapter in her book.

Adelia followed Tiera towards the ocean's floor. Adelia's eyes widened as she saw a coral reef full of vibrant oranges and yellows, like the ones in her room.

"I found some of the coral in your room here," Tiera explained.

Shocked at the world in front of her, Adelia swam to get a closer look.

"It's like a mini world! I have never seen so many fish in one place. Hi! Hi!" Adelia waved at the fish swimming in and out of the reef.

"Let's keep going. There's something else I want to show you before we head back home," Tiera continued swimming farther away from the tunnel.

Following Tiera, Adelia felt the cool sand as it became unsettled beneath her. She was amazed at how many creatures called it home. Adelia's books were filled with many interesting facts about the sea creatures that lived beneath the sand, but it was nothing compared to seeing it firsthand.

Tiera held Adelia's hand as they let a school of fish swim past over them. Adelia's eyes lit up in wonder as the light from above the sea caused the fish's fins to shimmer.

"Let's keep going, we are almost there," Tiera waved good-bye to the school of fish as they swam away.

Up ahead, Adelia saw tall green things flowing out of the sand floor. *She had read about them once. What were they called? Green weeds ... weeds...*

"It's a seaweed bed," Tiera reminded Adelia, "This is where I found you."

Stunned, Adelia looked at the green jungle before her.

"I found you right here, crying, and all alone," Tiera looked at Adelia; she was frozen. "Come here." Slowly, Adelia made her way to the spot where her mother had left her. Thought after thought raced through her mind. *Was her mother nearby? Could her father be waiting for her?*

Swimming to the sea floor, Adelia touched the spot where she had once laid abandoned, "Tiera, why did they leave me?"

Tiera laid beside Adelia, "I don't know, but I'm sure it was for a good reason."

Unsatisfied, Adelia looked into Tiera's eyes, "Sometimes I feel as if half of me is missing. I don't fit into your world, Tiera. I love you and mother, but I know there's something more for me out there. It's as if I've lost something but I can't remember what."

"I know and that's why we have given you the chance to explore this part of the ocean. Maybe you'll find a clue to where your mother is. And when you are older, you can decide if you want to leave the Western Sea Kingdom and go to the Northern Sea Kingdom. But for now, you are too young and the Northern Sea Kingdom is not safe. Especially since the crowning of their new king. Promise me Adelia that you won't lose that glimmer of hope that lies in your eyes," Tiera brushed back Adelia's hair from her face, "You'll find her someday, but for now we gotta start small."

"Thank you, Tiera, for everything," Adelia felt a new challenge birth inside her, "I am going to search every rock and seashell until I find her, starting here."

"I love your enthusiasm, Adelia, but how about we start tomorrow morning. I don't have school, so we can stay out here all day," Tiera grabbed Adelia's hand, "Plus, mother should be done with supper soon. We don't want to keep her waiting and cause her to worry."

"Ok, only if you promise to bring me out here tomorrow," Adelia said.

Tiera smiled, "I promise."

As they began to swim away, a sparkle caught Adelia's eyes. Swimming towards the light, Adelia sped up in excitement. A brown conch shell with blue, black, and white specks all around it poked up from the sand. Adelia sighed in awe. It was the most beautiful shell she had ever laid her eyes on.

"Tiera, look what I found!" Adelia raised the shell into the air.

"Adelia, where did you find this? This is a rare type of shell originally from the Northern Sea Kingdom!" Tiera grabbed the seashell and held it next to Adelia 's tail, "See how it matches your tail! Mother is going to freak out!"

Swimming as fast as they could the two mermaids swam back to the tunnel that would return them to the place they called home.

CHAPTER SIX

Captain Who?

Ten Years Since the Incident

Merena walked down the cold, stone hallway that led to Queen Ramona's room. She had walked this hallway many times fetching whatever the Queen's heart desired. It had been a decade since she had stepped foot outside of the castle. Arriving at Queen Ramona's door, Merena released a deep breath she hadn't realized she had been holding.

Slowly, Merena twisted the icy, cold doorknob. A cool breeze hit her face as the opened door revealed Queen Ramona pacing in front of her grand fireplace.

"Darling, Merena, I've been waiting for you! Can't you see I am stressed?" Queen Ramona marched over to Merena, "Do you know why I am stressed?"

Merena looked to the floor, "No, I am not aware of why you would be stressed. Is there anything I could do for you?"

Queen Ramona stomped her foot, "I have had it. In the past ten years I have yet to capture another mermaid like you. You say others like you exist, but where? I have tons of yellow, orange, violet, red, and even green-tailed mermaids, but you … you are different. None have the power you possess. Somehow after all these years you are still connected to the depths of the ocean."

"What do you mean?" Merena was taken by surprise.

"You don't think I know when you are happy, sad, or even angry? The ocean responds to you. And no one else, why?" Queen Ramona questioned.

"The ocean is not responding to me," Merena responded.

"Oh, but it does my dear. Do you know how I know?" Queen Ramona grasped Merena's arm, "It has stormed in *my* kingdom, the Kingdom of Hysteria, every day since you arrived. My people long for the days when they can sit on the beach and relax," Queen Ramona threw her hands up in frustration, "I long for the day when I can relax in the sun! But the ocean is longing for your return. Your kingdom is aching for you to save them from destruction."

Merena knew she was half right. Over the past year she had felt the burden of her lost kingdom fall upon her. The seas were unsteady, storms would last weeks, fishermen would bring in dead fish instead of live ones, and no one was happy.

"But you can't save your poor kingdom," Queen Ramona pointed at the mark that held Merena captive, "You belong to me."

Queen Ramona's icy glare seemed to stare straight into Merena's soul, "Now tell me where I can find others like you."

"You don't understand. Each kingdom that belongs to the ocean has a role to play. My kingdom is hidden for a reason, Queen Ramona. We blend into our surroundings, barely noticed, except when we are missing. My kingdom controls the balance of all things," Merena explained, "Without balance everything comes falling down. That includes the weather, but most importantly the spirits of the creatures that live in the ocean. Without balance, you will always feel like something is off or missing."

"What kind of talk is this, Merena?" Queen Ramona huffed in annoyance, "I just want to know where I can capture more mermaids like you."

Merena sighed, "I told you. My kind is born to blend in with the surroundings. You won't be able to find another mermaid like me."

"But I found you. Didn't I?" Queen Ramona grinned.

"I wasn't where I was supposed to be. I was out of my place. The ocean is where I belong and I left it," Merena's heart felt heavy, if only she had found a different favorite spot to escape to. Then maybe she would be playing with her twins right now.

"I will find more like you. That way you will stop torturing my kingdom with this terrible rain!" Queen Ramona stomped towards her closet, "Bring me my extra large crown! It is time to address the people!"

Nervous, Merena grabbed Queen Ramona's extremely large crown off a sapphire lace pillow. The crown was heavy from the hundreds of tiny diamonds that shined upon its surface. A pang of regret hovered over Merena's soul. *If only I had stayed beneath the waves, perhaps I would be wearing a crown as gorgeous as this right now...*

Patiently waiting for Queen Ramona to change clothes, Merena moved towards the windows at the far part of the room. Silently, she pulled back the elegant curtains to reveal the sea. A great sorrow fueled by anger swept over Merena. She wished with all her heart that she could break through the walls of her torture chamber and be free. Taking a last glance at the sea, Merena let go of the shaking curtain and regained her composure. *One day I'll escape. One day Queen Ramona's reign will fall.*

"Are you finished being emotional, Merena?" Queen Ramona mocked.

Shock flooded Merena's face. She hadn't realized Queen Ramona had been watching her.

"I am sorry. That was uncalled for.... Here is your staff," Merena bowed as she handed over the staff. As Queen Ramona's fingers touched the staff, the sapphire began to glow revealing a trapped conch shell within the precious stone.

"Grab my cap. I do not want it to drag the ground," Queen Ramona stormed forward. Struggling to grasp her cap, Merena followed Queen Ramona through her bedroom door.

Queen Ramona came to a halt, "James! Jaxson! I want to address the people from the balcony. Don't bother with setting up my throne room. I am too angry to sit!"

James and Jaxson popped their heads out of the door beside Queen Ramona.

"Yes, ma'am. Wait here while we summon the people," James said as he rushed towards the great window door.

Curiosity filled Merena. Since the time she had become Queen Ramona's handmaiden, she had not seen the outside world. Queen Ramona had always summoned the people in her throne room.

Jaxson rushed to Queen Ramona's side, "My queen, the people are ready."

"Then what are we waiting for?" Queen Ramona rushed forward, nearly dragging Merena behind her.

A gust of unfamiliar sounds rushed through Merena as Queen Ramona pushed open the glass doors. Resting Queen Ramona's cap on the floor, Merena took in the scene before her. Millions of people stood in black purple coats staring at their Queen. The people stood as straight as sticks but trembling in fear and exhaustion. A large cloud hovered over them, threatening to downpour on the homes of the people. Large tents covered what Merena believed to be a marketplace, but this was not the world Merena had first seen when she had arrived. Glancing around, she searched for a flying bird. The sky was empty, absent of any living creature.

She had read that the marketplace was always buzzing with excited people driven by passion to accomplish anything.

But the people that stood before her looked as if they hadn't dreamed in an entire lifetime. Even the children stood still without making a sound.

"My people, I know you are aching and are filled with sorrow. Every day is a terrible rainy day," Queen Ramona put on a face of pity, "I have been searching for a reason why this weather has been burdened upon us these past five years. And I feel I have discovered it!"

The people glanced around at each other, but none dared to break the silence.

"The ocean is angry with us! It feels we have taken something from it and given it nothing. It believes that it has the power to torture us. But do not fear! I have a plan to show the ocean that I am the Queen!" Queen Ramona raised her staff in the air.

Merena sighed. Queen Ramona didn't get it. It wasn't because Queen Ramona had taken Merena away from the ocean, but it was because the balance in the sea had been messed with. Burdened with the thought that it was her fault, Merena looked towards the direction of the sea. Her father had never entrusted anyone with his trident that held within it The Pearl Dust of Balance. If The pearl dust was truly missing from its place then that meant her kingdom was falling, her hope of her daughters living a peaceful life fading.

Taking Merena by surprise, Queen Ramona grabbed her by the hand, "My people, I have someone I'd like you to meet," Queen Ramona pushed Merena to the edge of the balcony, "This is your new official Captain of *The Siphon*. Aka, the newest mermaid hunter," Merena's body turned to stone. *What was Queen Ramona talking about? She would never capture her own kind.*

Merena turned to face Queen Ramona, "I will not hunt mermaids."

Queen Ramona turned Merena back towards the crowd and pulled her in close, "Smile and wave…. You will do whatever

I wish." Struggling to loosen Queen Ramona's grasp, Merena feared she would never escape her evilness.

"Enough!" Queen Ramona hit her staff to the ground, sending pain through Merena's arm.

Grabbing Merena's hand, Queen Ramona pointed at the glowing conch shell upon Merena's skin, "Next time you have second thoughts about what I command upon you, I will make your whole body crumble in pain."

Queen Ramona glared at Merena before she put on a smile and looked at her citizens, "Meet Merena. She is going to catch those monsters that lurk in our waters. And if she fails, we will have her to blame for our misery." The ground shook in response to the crowd's cheers.

Queen Ramona pulled Merena into the castle, "Go get lunch ready and then we talk more about your ... promotion."

Queen Ramona shoved past Merena, leaving her alone, standing in the hallway with her thoughts.

Merena tried to move but, at the moment, she couldn't even breathe. She had too many questions. *Was she going to have to kill her ocean friends? What even is a captain of the… What was it Queen Ramona had said?*

Making her way to the royal kitchen, Merena let her mind wander. *Would she still be Queen Ramona's handmaiden? Would she have to sail a ship?* Merena grabbed a pan and began making Queen Ramona's pancake lunch. *What will happen to me if I don't capture my friends?*

Merena winced as some grease hit her hand, reminding her of the power Queen Ramona had over her. Adding some blueberries to Queen Ramona's pancakes, Merena focused on the task at hand. But it was an ill effort. Worry filled her mind. The idea of not knowing what was to come overtook her. She badly wanted to curl up in her bed and cry. Shaking, Merena poured Queen Ramona's fresh Pomegranate Juice into a tall purple, sapphire glass. A sudden thought of hope crossed her mind, *Would she get to touch the ocean once more? Maybe even go for a swim? Could this be her chance to see her daughters?*

Merena finished making the Queen's lunch and started her long-dreaded walk back towards Queen Ramona's room. Each step felt like a page turning in her book. A new chapter for her was beginning. Would it be for the best or turn her bad dreams into a nightmare?

CHAPTER SEVEN

A Terrible Fate

When Merena arrived at the Queen's bedroom door, she was shocked to see it slightly open. Gently, Merena pushed open the large door to find Queen Ramona sitting at her grand seat by the fireplace. She was speaking with another servant.

Glancing towards Merena, Queen Ramona smiled, "I see you have brought me my lunch. Boy, do I love pancakes for lunch... Please come sit and talk with us."

Merena laid Queen Ramona's lunch tray, full of breakfast foods, upon the Queen's lap and took her place beside a servant Merena had never seen before. She had wavy and vibrate orange hair that was halfway pulled back. Her eyes were a dark green that almost seemed hazel. Her dress was the normal dull green.

"Merena, I'd like you to meet, Camilla," Queen Ramona said with her mouth full, "She is going to be my new hand-maiden." The young servant nodded in fear. She was another lost girl unsure of her future.

Queen Ramona gulped down her juice and wiped her face before she shoved her tray across the table between the servants and the queen.

"Camilla, why don't you go wash my plates and then prepare my gown for tonight's dinner. I have some important business to discuss with my former handmaiden," Queen Ramona said. The young servant nearly ran out of the room with the tray of dirty dishes.

"Now that we are alone, tell me, are you excited?" Queen Ramona leaned in as if she wanted to hear everything Merena had to say. Merena searched for words. *Was she excited to possibly see the ocean again? Maybe. Was she excited to hunt down her kind? Never.* Merena took a deep breath and stared at the now impatient looking Queen Ramona.

"I am excited to … see the ocean again, I guess," Merena stumbled to find more to say, "I'm just not sure what else I should be excited for."

"My dear child, you will get to set sail on a big ship and find your friends and family. You'll get to tell about the amazing life you've lived here. They all want to be up here on land, you know. You will be doing them a favor by … by providing them with transportation to the mainland," Queen Ramona smiled, "What do you say?"

Frustration filled Merena. Queen Ramona was speaking as if her life was amazing here. Like Merena wanted to bring her family here, the place she longed to escape.

"I do not love it here. Why would I want to bring my family to a place where they would spend the rest of their lives trapped?" Merena questioned.

Queen Ramona seemed disgusted, "You don't love it here? I provide you a place to stay and sleep. In my opinion, that's better than nothing… It's way better than, perhaps, never seeing your daughters again."

"Better than nothing? You took me away from my home. You took me away from my daughters!" Merena cried, "Why would I ever want to take away their dreams like you did to me?"

"I knew it!" Queen Ramona laughed, "You're so protective of your little home because of your kids. Well, listen to me, fish, you will keep bringing me more mermaids until this storm that rules my kingdom subsides."

"I can't..." Merena started.

"No, you can, and you will. You are the new Captain of *The Siphon*. The biggest ship in the northern hemisphere. You will spend your days at sea bringing me the creatures that have cursed my kingdom and if you don't..." Queen Ramona smirked, "Like I said the kingdom will blame you for our troubles."

Queen Ramona stood up and faced the fireplace, "Now, go and get some rest. Your new uniform will be waiting on your bed in the morning. I truly hope your life at sea serves you well..." Queen Ramona turned away from the fire, "Oh, I almost forgot. Camilla and I will be joining you on your first three-month voyage. I want to make sure you understand everything about your new job. Plus, since I won't be captain, it will be like a free cruise for me,,, We set sail in one week."

Queen Ramona left Merena sitting in the room staring at the fire. The flames seemed to grow, anger and fear raging. Merena felt herself approaching the fire, grabbing the water bucket beside it, as she tossed the water upon it, letting the light of the room leave her as well. Focusing on the small light that shone from the outside of the door, Merena left Queen Ramona's room, trying to focus on the light she still had in her own life. The light that came from her love for her husband and her twins, her twins who she prayed were enjoying their lives under the sea.

CHAPTER EIGHT

Becoming a Pirate

The next morning, Merena woke with a start as a young teen with brunette pigtails tapped on her shoulder. The young teen looked like a pirate. She was wearing a red and black dress that had puffy shirt sleeves. To complete the outfit, a red bandana was wrapped around her head and a sword swung at her side. Merena did not think much about it due to the fact she had just awakened.

"Captain Merena, it is time for you to get dressed," the young teen nodded towards Merena's clothes at the end of the bed. Sitting up, Merena looked around. *What time was it? The sun hadn't even woken up yet. So much for that beauty sleep Queen Ramona had told her to get.*

The floor was icy cold to her feet as she stood up from her bed. Half awake, Merena grabbed her clothes and tiptoed to the servant bathroom.

Blinded by the bright bathroom light, Merena went into one of the stalls to change. The teen who had awakened her patiently waited outside for Merena.

Merena glanced at her side and sighed, more scars had begun to appear upon her skin. Counting over a dozen more since the first two had appeared, Merena wanted with all her might to challenge whoever had taken her kingdom. However, she was helpless as long as she was under the control of Queen Ramona. Her fingertips rubbed across the scar of her father, causing her body to ache. Whether the pain was physical or mental, she knew that she deserved it. Merena felt like their deaths were her fault. If only she had been there, maybe she could have done something to stop the evil one.

"Um, is anyone out there?" Merena questioned as she zipped up the last part of her outfit.

"I am," the young teen said, "Is everything ok?"

Opening the stall door, Merena examined herself in the mirror, "I think I have the wrong outfit." Merena was wearing a white blouse over the shoulder shirt with a brown leather vest that was tightened down the middle. She had a dark blue skirt that rippled like a curtain. It was short in the front, but the tail fell long in the back. Tall leather heel boots came high up on her leg.

"Wow! You look so cool, Captain Merena," the girl expressed, "But your outfit isn't complete yet. Come sit." The girl directed Merena towards a chair in front of the mirror.

Reluctantly, Merena sat in the chair, "I don't understand what's going on. Why do you keep calling me Captain?"

The girl quickly applied what felt like a pound of makeup on Merena's face. She brushed Merena's hair before she started to braid small sections of Merena's wavy beach black hair.

"You are our new captain. It looks like you've got a lot to learn. By the way, I'm Adrie, your first mate," Adrie smiled, "I've been at sea all my life. Don't worry, I will teach you everything I know about being a pirate."

Merena jumped, "A pirate!" Suddenly the outfit and makeup started to make sense.

"Yeah, a pirate. Now sit down and let me finish. You don't want to address your crew looking like a maid," Adrie attached large gold jewelry all over Merena's outfit, including: gold strings in her hair, gold hoop earrings, gold chains, and a gold necklace. Adrie started to take Merena's locket off, but Merena slapped her hand away.

"Please, can I keep this on?" Merena held the locket in her hand.

Adrie stared at her for a second, "Hum, let me see? May I?" Adrie touched the locket, and Merena reluctantly let her take it off. Merena watched Adrie braid the necklace with a gold lace and then attach it to the side of her skirt.

"There. Now if that's not stylish then I don't know what it is," Adrie grabbed a pirate's hat from the bathroom counter, "Just one more thing." Adrie sat the silky blue pirate's hat upon Merena's head. Merena looked at the stranger in the mirror. The makeup made her look fierce and the outfit made the impression that she was a strong leader. But to Merena this just felt like a super cool outfit, not who she was about to become.

"What have I gotten myself into?" Merena mumbled.

"A whole new life of fighting pirates, stealing gold, and capturing creatures from below. Here!" Adrie drew a long, sharp sword from her side. Grabbing the leather blue handle, Merena felt sick. *Fighting with this? How would I do that?*

As if she had read Merena's mind, Adrie sighed, "You don't know how to use a sword? I have less to work with than I thought."

Adrie once again examined Merena from head to toe, "Well, you look like a pirate now, but you are going to need way more than that to win the hearts of your crew. We are going to have to train day in and day out. Seashells, we only have one week to get you ready."

"Adrie, I don't know about this. I am not a pirate," Merena shook her head.

"I know," Adrie placed the sword in the slot on the side of Merena's dress, "If you are what I think you are, then you are quite the opposite," Adrie winked as she walked towards the bathroom door. Merena reluctantly followed this young teen who seemed to know more about her future than she did.

CHAPTER NINE

Swords and More

Adrie led Merena down a hidden passageway like the one Merena had first entered the day she had been captured. Silently hoping for it to lead outside of the castle, Merena tried to see a light at the end of the tunnel. Nothing yet.

"So, how long have you been … a pirate?" Merena questioned.

"All my life, my parents died when I was really young and my uncle, the late sea captain of The Siphon, took me in," Adrie explained.

Merena nearly stumbled to the ground. *Had her uncle died because he was the captain?*

"My uncle was thrown overboard by an enemy crew after he was captured," Adrie sighed, "He was like a father to me, but that's how this business works."

Merena felt sick. *Queen Ramona was sending her to her death. There was no way she would survive if that seasoned pirate couldn't survive.*

As if reading Merena's mind, Adrie continued, "My uncle was old and getting cocky. He thought it would be fun to show the crew that he could escape being held hostage … Lesson number one: a cocky pirate is a dead pirate."

Merena nervously smiled. This was going to be quite the adventure. A bright light came into Merena's vision up ahead. Adrie picked up their pace until they basically ran out of the cave and onto a sandy beach, exactly like the one Merena had first walked on when she arrived. Nearly out of breath, Merena stopped to pick up a small cerith shell. It was nothing like the ones she used to collect under the sea, but it was still a shell. Splashing into the ocean, Merena felt like a sponge, soaking in all of the water. The waves were a relief to the stress she had been under for the past decade.

"Merena, we don't have time for fun and games. I've got to get you ready to become the captain," Adrie drew a sword from her side. Staring at the sword, Merena felt the one by her side. *Did she want me to fight her?*

"Come on. Bring out your sword just like I did," Adrie beckoned Merena. Walking up to Adrie, Merena drew her sword. It was heavier than she thought it was going to be.

Adrie lifted Merena's sword up with hers and said, "Swing at me." Merena lifted her sword up and swung, but only to find that Adrie was strong. She pushed Merena back, sending her smashing into the sand. Looking up in defeat, Merena sighed.

"Get up and swing at me again!" Adrie commanded.

Merena wiped the sand off her knees and prepared to swing again. This time Adrie moved out of the way. Merena felt the weight of the sword pull her forward sending her face first into the sand. A burning sensation filled her eyes. *How am I going to ever get good at this?*

"Again!" Adrie poked Merena with her sword, "Let's go!"

When did this girl get so bossy? Standing up, Merena looked at Adrie before she prepared to swing again. *This was going to be a long week.*

Merena ran her hands through the damp sand that surrounded her as the sun set. Her whole body ached from her training. The constant work from sunrise to sunset for the past six days was starting to get to Merena. These past few days had better pay off because no matter what, tomorrow she had to be ready.

"Hey, don't worry about it. The crew is going to love you," Adrie gracefully fell beside Merena, "You didn't even faceplant once today."

Merena laughed. That was true, she was getting pretty good with a sword. The gun was another story, however. She wasn't a pro yet, but she wasn't an amateur either.

"Adrie, the last time I watched a sunset this beautiful I was way out in the ocean," Merena sighed, "The moment before the storm."

"Sunsets are always the prettiest when you're on the water," Adrie continued, "Merena, are you ready for our final mini-pirate lesson?"

"Yes," Merena watched the sun escape below the horizon.

"Today's lesson is on pirate legends. Remember how I explained to you that pirates use treasure maps to either direct them back to their loot or send other pirates on wild goose chases?" Adrie explained, "One of my favorite pirate legends would be about Madame Klamp. She was fierce, owning one thousand eight hundred ships and seventy thousand men. She ruled the seas by demanding protection money from coastal communities, attacking ships, and even kidnapping seven of Ramona's grand sailors! She was in charge of a huge smuggling operation. And it was said that all throughout the northern hemisphere she has buried treasure. And it just so happens that my uncle found a map that he believed to be hers!"

Merena felt the cool breeze send chills down her bones.

"Can you imagine how rich we would be?" Adrie looked Merena in the eye, "There's just one catch that has kept so many pirates from getting their hands on the loot."

Merena sighed. *Why was there always a catch?*

"The legend says that Madame Klamp had made friends with mermaids. It is said that those mermaids were of royal blood and possessed power. They enchanted her treasure so that only Madame Klamp and the royal family would be able to access it," Adrie stood up and grabbed Merena's hand, "Please tell me you're royal!" Merena felt shocked. She hadn't exactly told Adrie that she was a mermaid.

"How did you know I was a mermaid?" Merena questioned.

Adrie jumped with excitement, "I had my assumptions but you just confirmed them! I can't believe I am talking to a real life mermaid. You guys are legends too you know! There are tons of stories about mermaid treasure! And now that you're our captain we can find them all!"

"I don't want to hurt anyone, but I guess it would be fun to go on a treasure hunt," Merena followed Adrie down the sandy beach.

"Merena, sometimes people are born into a life that they don't want. While others have their life flip around into something they never dreamed was possible. Good or bad. You've just got to go where the waves take you. No matter if you think it's the right way or not. You have to trust the thing that gives you life," Adrie smiled.

Merena leaned down to pick up a small blue coquina shell, "I know exactly what you mean."

"You never answered my question about you being royal," Adrie had an eager look in her eyes. Merena tried to fight the bad memories that were racing through her mind.

"I am. I am ... was the soon to be Queen of the Northern Sea Kingdom," Merena felt a tear escape her eyes. *Oh, how I miss the sea.*

"If you don't mind me asking, what happened?" Adrie inquired.

"About my kingdom? Well, it's still there falling apart without a ruler," Merena explained.

"How do you know?" asked Adrie.

"The seas are unbalanced. Balance is what my kingdom controls. These storms and loss of fish is just a prime example of the destruction my kingdom is facing," Merena held her locket that swung on her side.

Adrie glanced at Merena's legs, "What about your tail?"

"Queen Ramona took it away. She took me away," Merena felt tears forming in her eyes, "She took everything away."

"I'm sorry," Adrie touched Merena's hand, "Maybe one of the legends has something about getting a mermaid's tail back. I know there's one about a trident." Fear bolted through Merena. The last time she had heard the word trident was the day her parents died.

"Merena, are you ok? Is it something I said," Adrie had a worried look on her face.

Realizing she had stopped walking, Merena sped up her pace, "It's just something in my past." Putting a smile on her face, Merena continued, "I do hope we can find a way to get my tail back. It might be hard with Queen Ramona on the ship."

Adrie laughed, "Queen Ramona won't be on the ship for more than three weeks. She absolutely can't stand it. She hates not being in her castle. If you show her you are a great captain, she'll leave us alone." A spark of hope swept through Merena. Maybe she was a step closer to regaining her tail. But deep in her mind she knew that Queen Ramona would never truly leave her alone as long as she bore the mark upon her skin.

Shaking the thought away, Merena smiled, "Enough about me and more about you Adrie."

"Ok, well, I've lived a pretty adventurous life," Adrie started walking faster, "I grew up fighting for what I wanted and taking what I needed. It's what you have to do to survive, especially when you live with a bunch of boys."

"Sounds exciting," Merena laughed nervously knowing this was going to be her life soon. Adrie stopped suddenly.

"Oh, I almost forgot, instead of sleeping in the cave like we've been doing, we are going to sleep on *The Siphon*," Adrie turned down a dock. Merena's heart began to race as a giant ship came into view. It was hard to see its beauty because the sun had faded away and the darkness had taken over, but she could tell that it was huge.

"Is the pirate crew … in there?" Merena stopped before going up the ramp that led to the main deck of the ship.

"Of course not. They're out and about the town," Adrie continued up the steep ramp, "Plus no one goes into the captain's quarters but the captain and his … or her first mate. Which is you and me," Merena nodded. She wished she could see what the ship really looked like, but it was too dark. Climbing onto the ship, Merena felt the cool breeze blow her hair in the wind. It was one of the things she had missed during the time she had been locked away.

Each step that Adrie and Merena made caused the boat to moan. It made Merena feel eerie as if someone was watching her. Adrie walked across the wooden vessel and towards a large door. She grabbed what Merena assumed was a lighter and lit two torches on each end of the door. Grabbing one of the torches, she flung open the door.

"Wow!" Merena explained as the light revealed a giant room with a desk, shelves of books, and a bed that went into the wall, "It's so big!"

"Welcome to your new room!" Adrie explained, "You can sleep here tonight and when the sun rises tomorrow you will meet your crew. And I'll show you around the ship."

"Where will you stay?" Merena sat down on the springy bed.

Adrie laughed, "Don't worry, this is my home. I've got a place to stay. I can't wait till you get a taste of this life!"

Adrie skipped towards the door before turning back towards Merena, "Oh, and remember to keep your sword and gun nearby. You never know who might want to join us on *The Siphon.*" A nervous laugh escaped Merena. *Was she kidding? Probably...*

Merena laid her head down on the stiff pillow. *At least this was better than serving Queen Ramona morning and night.* Staring at the wood above her, Merena let herself drift off to sleep.

CHAPTER TEN

Bon Voyage

Swush! Merena woke up to the sound of water hitting the side of the boat. Hurriedly Merena got dressed for the day. She put on her full pirate outfit. The past few days she had skipped the cap, the hat, and a bit of the jewelry, but she knew that today she'd need to look her best. Sitting at a mirror on the far end of the room, Merena fixed her hair like Adrie had done the first day they had met.

Knock! Knock! Merena nearly fell off her seat as Adrie came strolling in.

"Need any help, Captain?" Adrie was already dressed and ready for the day.

Seeing the embarrassment on Merena's face, Adrie started applying Merena's makeup, "Don't worry you'll get the hang of it… Perfect!" Adrie placed Merena's hat on her head as Merena attached her jewelry as Adrie had instructed her to. Standing up, Merena glanced at herself in the mirror. She sure looked like a pirate, she had trained like a pirate, and now it was time to see if she could be a pirate.

"Now you remember the phrases I taught you during the second lesson?" Adrie said as she adjusted her dress in the mirror, "You're about to hear a lot more of it from the guys outside. Oh, and a few of them have patched eyes, scars in odd places, peg legs, and hooks for hands. They are pretty proud of them so don't be afraid to compliment them."

Merena just shook her head and tried to remember the phrase Adrie had told her to say when she first met the crew.

"Now you are going to walk with confidence out this door and up the stairs to the top deck," Adrie opened the door, "Here we go."

Merena felt shaky but she pushed through it, walking with more confidence with each step, barely noticing the looks on the crew's faces.

Standing on the top deck, Merena glanced around. She hadn't realized how high up she was. She felt like she was a thousand stories up. The pirates before her were a sight to see. Adrie was right. They all had some sort of battle scar from two peg legs to a giant hook on their hand.

Merena took a deep breath before speaking, "Ahoy mateys! I am ye's new cap'n. I'm proud to be able to serve ye on me *The Siphon*," Merena glanced over at Adrie hoping she had said everything right. At least the pirates didn't look like they wanted to kill her.

Adrie stepped up beside Merena, "Alrighty crew introduce one's self!"

"I'm the swabby of this ye ship. I mop and clean the decks of *The Siphon*. My name is Ganon Nail Bird," a short pirate with a large eye patch said.

A younger looking pirate with a peg leg stepped forward, "I'm the ship's carpenter and me name's Nadan Savage Blade."

"I'm the pilot and me name's Hayby Hook Shell. I guide *The Siphon* to treasure, but it looks like I found one right in front of me," winked a tall hook handed pirate.

Merena tried to keep a confident and power look upon her face as each pirate introduced himself. She did not want to get on the wrong foot with any of these pirates. They would surely destroy her in an instant. Merena felt a hook rub against her face causing her to stand as still as possible.

"How did a pretty maiden like yourself become our new cap'n," the pirate who owned the hook hand asked from behind Merena, "You're absolutely perfect, unlike our Adrie here who has a scar right down her arm," Merena noticed Adrie pull her sleeves down as she turned red. *I guess girl pirates aren't as proud of their scars as the men.*

"But I think ye will do. You are quite a catch," the pirate turned her around and scanned her from head to toe. Merena noticed that he had scars all over his body and it seemed he liked gold jewelry. He had it everywhere from his ears to his boots. It was a little much in Merena's opinion.

"Tell me your name," Merena commanded.

The pirate laughed, "Lody Shark Tooth me name and remind me of your's cap'n."

"Cap'n Merena is me name," Merena gave a shot at her accent.

"Enough!" Adrie shouted, "Get to work boys, we set sail at noon. Remember the Queen will be joining us. So, please be on your best behavior." Adrie led Merena back down to the main deck. A crooked smile appeared across Hayby Hook Shell's face as Merena left him standing by the boat's wheel.

Shutting the door to the captain's quarters Merena let out a deep breath, "Wow, you weren't kidding when you said they were intimidating. I don't know if I can handle all of them plus Queen Ramona on this boat!"

"You're doing fine. Now you remember the pirate code I spoke to you about?" Adrie grabbed a scroll off the desk in the middle of the room.

"Yeah, the one with the rules about the division of treasure, discipline, and compensation of an injured pirate," Merena recalled.

"Well, here it is," Adrie handed Merena the scroll.

It read:

"Every crewmate shall have an equal vote in the affairs of the moment."

"The lights and candles shall be put out at eight at night, and if any of the crew desire to go out after that hour they shall do so in the dark."

"Each crewmate shall keep his piece, cutlass, and pistols at all times clean and ready for action."

"He or she that shall desert the ship or his or her quarters in the time of battle shall be punished by death."

"The Captain and First Mate shall receive two shares of a prize: the master, boatswain, and gunner shall receive one share and a half, and the other officers will receive one and a quarter of the prize."

"The musicians shall have rest on the Sabbath Day but shall receive no rest during the other six days and nights. Unless they are given special favor by the captain."

"You will need to memorize this," Adrie explained, "The crew will be busy until we set sail. I arranged it that way so we can plan where we will be heading. It's up to you but I'm hoping you will want to search for Madame Klamp's treasure." Adrie pulled out a book from the largest bookcase, causing a hidden compartment to open on the desk in the middle. Amazed, Merena looked to Adrie for an explanation.

"Pirates, especially my uncle, have many secrets. We don't trust anyone, and neither should you," Adrie pulled out a large, aging paper from the compartment. She cleared off the desk before she spread the treasure map across it, "Here it is. Are you up for the challenge, Captain?"

"I am," feeling adventurous, Merena touched the map, "First stop is Megalodon Island." Merena smiled as yet another memory popped into her mind.

"Have you ever met a Megalodon, Merena?" Adrie asked, "They are assumed to be dead."

Merena laughed, "Megalodons dead? No, they are definitely alive. Their attitude is almost as big as their size. It's one of the few sea creatures I tend to stay away from. They won't bother us though."

Merena thought she saw a glimpse of fear in Adrie's eyes, "How do you know?"

"They can't injure mermaids. A long time ago, a megalodon made a promise to never hurt a fellow mermaid if mermaids would promise to let the Megalodons mind their own business. The only thing that can change that is if they are controlled by the trident," Merena assured Adrie, "And plus they hibernate during this time of year."

Adrie let out a sigh of relief, "I'm glad. Sharks are by far my least favorite animals. Especially the ones that can eat me in one bite. Now that we know where we are going, let's talk about Queen Ramona's orders."

"Her orders to capture mermaids?" Merena's heart quickened. She'd almost forgotten that she was going to have to do that.

Adrie nodded, "Where will we find them?" Scanning the map, Merena felt her heart pounding in her chest. *What will happen if she leads them on a wild goose chase?* She only had to last three weeks with Queen Ramona.

"What will happen to the mermaids we catch? Is there any way around it?" Merena questioned.

"You heard Queen Ramona. She blames you for everything bad that has happened in our kingdom. Whether that means being imprisoned for life or the death penalty, I'm not sure," Adrie gave Merena a reassuring smile, "What's a few more mermaids if we can find a way to free them all?" The thought struck Merena like a giant wave. *Free all the mermaids?*

"So, you're saying we play along with Queen Ramona's plan until we find a way to free all the mermaids under her control?" Merena started to scan the map before her.

Adrie grinned, "And taking some treasure at the same time... So, where will we find the mermaids?"

"Here," Merena reluctantly pointed northwest towards the middle of the ocean, "A lot of mermaids tend to explore in this area. They sometimes are brave enough to swim near ships." A guilty feeling swept over Merena and she prayed that she had not betrayed her merfolk.

"Will they be mermaids like you?" Adrie questioned as she began to calculate the distance from Megalodon Island to the area Merena had pointed at.

"You mean mermaids from the Northern Sea Kingdom?" Merena watched Adrie work.

"I mean, will they look like you? That's what Queen Ramona wants," Adrie put her pencil down and examined her work.

Merena tried to understand the weird lines she had drawn on the map, "Um, all mermaids look extremely different. Their skin, hair, and eyes are all unique to each mermaid. Families tend to look alike, just like humans. However, there are only four types of tails. The reason is due to the different water climates. My tail was deep ocean blue. My kingdom was cold and deeper in the ocean than the other three kingdoms. So, our tails tend to blend into the ocean, a way of camouflage. That's why it's so rare to catch mermaids from the Northern Sea Kingdom.

Adrie's eyes were bursting with curiosity, "What about the other kingdoms?"

"The kingdom nearest to the surface, their tails are yellow and orange, the kingdom near the volcanoes have tails that are reds and pinks. And lastly, the kingdom full of vegetation has mermaids with green tails," Merena explained.

"Wow," Adrie said in awe, "That's amazing."

"Anything else we need to do?" Merena asked.

Adrie shook her head, "We just have to…" a loud trumpet noise interrupted Adrie. "Speaking of the Queen." Merena felt her legs go numb. It had been an amazing past few days without having to worry about Queen Ramona. Adrie shoved open the captain's door. Walking outside, Merena felt as if tiny little fish were biting her. Looking up in confusion, she glanced at Adrie for an explanation.

"I know it's weird. It hasn't rained for the past week," Adrie walked over to the edge of the boat. *So, this is rain.* The storm clouds had been threatening all week and it looked like today it was going to pour.

"Eh, it's raining! Take me to my room now! CAMILLA, WHY DON'T YOU HAVE THE UMBRELLA OPENED YET! IT'S NOT ROCKET SCIENCE!" Queen Ramona screamed. Merena quickly joined Adrie who was now bowing before Queen Ramona.

Poor Camilla, Merena thought as the girl struggled to open the umbrella. Queen Ramona didn't even care to glance towards Merena as she stomped towards the opposite side of the ship. Slamming the door to what Merena assumed was Queen Ramona's room, Queen Ramona let out a cry of disgust, "I hate water!"

Adrie elbowed Merena, "See, I told you she won't last long," Adrie stepped up on a barrel and reached out her hand to Merena, "Let's call the crew to order." Stepping up upon the barrel, Merena felt unsteady. Adrie nudged Merena to the edge of the barrel. Taking a deep breath, Merena shouted, "It's time to set sail. Everyone to their positions!"

"Aye, aye Captain!" the crew shouted. Merena glanced around as everyone began doing something different. She felt like she was the only one unsure of what to do.

"You won't have many duties until we catch a mermaid or are in battle," Adrie explained as she hopped down from the barrel, "Right now you can get to know the crew and make sure everyone's doing their job. I've got to go let Hayby Hook Shell know our course." And with that Adrie left Merena alone. Stepping down from the barrel, Merena took a deep breath before she continued her new duties as Captain of *The Siphon*.

CHAPTER ELEVEN

One's Loss Is Another's Gain

Thunder roared above the sea as Adelia searched through the green seaweed where she had been found as a merbaby. The ocean had become her new playground over the past three weeks. Her young eyes were filled with wonder, hope, and joy. As Adelia felt the sharp edges of broken seashells between her fingers, she searched the sand beneath her. Today she was solely focusing on finding a clue as to why her mother and father had left her.

"Adelia you've searched there a million times. Don't you want to look elsewhere?" Tiera questioned.

Adelia nodded, there was one place she wanted to visit. Glancing up, Adelia kicked her tail against the sand as she burst off like a rocket, feeling the water brush past her face and Adelia swam towards the surface. Just as she was about to break through the barrier, she felt something grab her tail and pull her back. A moment of fear rushed through Adelia. But it vanished quickly at the realization that it was only Tiera.

Adelia sighed, "You scared me!"

"I scared you! You know we can't leave the water!" Adelia watched as Tiera's face turned a crimson red.

"I'm sorry," Adelia looked at the surface above. She was inches from touching another world, "I just wanted to see what it was like up there."

A longing look escaped Tiera's eyes, "I've always wanted to too..."

Reluctantly Tiera reached her hand up, stopping right before the surface, "Do you promise not to tell Mom? It will only be a second."

"I promise ... you can go first," Adelia felt her body bubble with excitement. Patiently waiting, Adelia watched Tiera reach her hand through the surface. A smile transformed upon Tiera's face as she broke through the barrier that separated the sea from the sky. Not waiting another minute, Adelia felt the sea burst open around her as she saw the air surrounding her. Scanning the sky above, Adelia leaped into the air like a dolphin, "I feel so free!"

Tiera grabbed her hand, "Look at the world out there! What do you think is behind that line where the sea meets the sky!"

"I wish we could go there!" Adelia said with a longing glance. The sea began to become unsteady as the sun began to set.

Tiera pulled Adelia back under water, "Let's come back tomorrow when we can see the sun set and rise!" Adelia hugged Tiera before glancing at the new world she had discovered.

"Evalyn," Lulu touched her right fin against Evalyn's shoulder. Opening her eyes, Evalyn stretched her tired arms. She had stayed up late playing her conch shell.

"Morning Lulu!" Evalyn twirled in the air and shook her hair wildly, in an attempt to wake herself up.

"Guess what we will be doing today?" Grabbing Evalyn into her arms, Lulu brought her back towards the sea floor.

"What?" Evalyn's crystal eyes glazed up in wonder.

Lulu began to swim towards the exit of the cave, "We think it's time you go for a swim with the pod and maybe even start working on your jumps!"

Excitement filled her whole body. She had been waiting for a chance to swim with the pod ever since she could remember.

Swimming ahead of Lulu, Evalyn felt a huge smile escape her face, "Thank you so much!"

"Since it's your first time going towards the surface, hold on to my fin, little one," Lulu nodded.

Evalyn felt Lulu's smooth skin run against hers as she grabbed hold. A gust of water hit her face as Lulu burst towards the sky. The water rushed past Evalyn at lightning speed. As they neared the surface, Evalyn held on tighter. A spark of fear went through her body as the unexplored world came into view. Closing her eyes, she felt the water burst off her skin and into multiple directions. Opening her eyes, Evalyn felt her finger begin to slip from Lulu's fin. The light air seemed to pull her away and back towards the water.

Splash! Skin stinging, Evalyn took a deep breath and relaxed before poking her head back up above the surface. Taking in the new world around her, Evalyn's eyes scanned the dark, fluffy objects floating above her. Wishing she could touch them, Evalyn reached as high as she could. *I guess I'll always be cut off from a world I'll never get to explore.*

"It's amazing," Evalyn let out a sigh of wonder.

"Come on, let's swim a little further," Lulu poked her head above the surface.

Spinning in a circle, Evalyn looked as far as she could towards where the sea met the sky.

"Lulu look!" Evalyn pointed towards the West, "Is that mermaids?"

A shocked look came over Lulu's face, but before she could focus on the mermaids ahead, the sea began to rumble.

"Let's go Evalyn," Lulu grabbed Evalyn 's arm. Watching the tails of the two mermaids disappear under the waves, Evalyn reluctantly obeyed Lulu. *What if that had been her mom?*

One Week Later

Adelia scanned the sky above her as she floated on her back. Tonight, the clouds had parted and the sun shone in the distance. An array of colors filled Adelia 's vision as the sun started to make its way towards the horizon. Tiera had been on vacation from school this week and the two mergirls had decided they would secretly explore the land above. They never went far and were cautious to stay far away from the mainland.

Glancing at Tiera, Adelia smiled at how peaceful she looked as she let the waves move her. Adelia watched Tiera close her eyes. Her blond hair spread out like jelly fish. Pushing her hair out like Tiera's, Adelia relaxed into the ocean. She felt refreshed as the water splashed against her tail. Her eyes closed and any tension left in her body released. Smiling, Tiera let her mind wander.

A vision of a young merwoman with dark hair and a dark blue tail filled Adelia's mind. There was a slight glow that surrounded the mermaid. The young mermaid's crystal eyes began to shine as she floated nearer to Adelia.

"Where are you, Nanami? Please help me, Nanami. I need you," The mermaid in the vision reached for Adelia. Adelia felt her heart rising as questions flooded her mind. *Who was this mermaid? Why is she calling Nanami?* Adelia tried to grab the mermaid but it was as if she had been turned to stone.

She couldn't move. The vision of the mermaid began to fade as she spoke the words, "I will find you and Syrena. One day we will be a family again," and then all was dark.

Lost and confused, Adelia opened her eyes. Fear filled her little body as she realized that the sun had escaped beyond the horizon and the waves had begun to increase. Thunder shook the sea as Adelia searched for Tiera. Wincing as the rain flooded her eyes, Adelia dived into the sea. Tiera was nowhere to be found.

"Tiera!" Adelia burst back above the roaring waves. Vision blurry from tears, Adelia listened for Tiera.

At first she heard nothing, but then, "Help me, Adelia! Help me!" Turning around Adelia felt as if her worst nightmare had come true. A large pirate ship was struggling through the waves in the distance. A large net was being reeled in. Panic swept over Adelia as she realized that Tiera was fighting to escape the large fish net. *What was she to do?*

Swimming through the waves, Adelia approached the ship. *She had to do something.* She felt her body turn to ice as the world around her began to move in slow motion. She locked eyes with a pirate. She was holding on to the railing of the vessel, her long dark hair flowing in the wind. To Adelia it seemed like her eyes were glowing. Adelia felt as if she had seen those crystal eyes before. The vision. She was the mermaid from her vision! *Who was she?*

Adelia noticed a spark of fear in the woman's eyes as she began to beckon Adelia away.

"*Swim away,*" her mouth beckoned, "*I'll protect your friend.*" Shocked that she could hear the mysterious woman from this far out at sea, Adelia took one last glance at the now limp Tiera. Adelia obeyed the pirate. Diving into the sea, Adelia 's mind raced. *What was she going to tell her Mom? Would she ever see Tiera again? Who was that mermaid in her dreams? Were the mermaid and the pirate the same person?*

The water rushed past Adelia as she zoomed through the waters and back into the cave entrance. She had to warn the other mermaids that the humans were venturing closer to the kingdom. Bursting into her room, Adelia nearly crashed into her neon orange coral decor.

Fear fueled her brain as she jerked open her shell door, "Mom!" Not slowing her pace, Adelia swam through the hallway and into the kitchen to meet six confused eyes.

❧

Gusts of wind pounded against Merena's body, throwing her every which way. Her skin tore as she felt her hand slip down a thick, course rope. Making her way towards the edge of the boat, her body struggled against the waves that seemed to be attacking *The Siphon*. Her pirate crew began to shout sounds of joy as James and Jaxon lowered their nets upon deck. Squinting to see the nets, Merena feared they had caught the northern mermaid she had just seen moments before. Praying she was mistaken and that they had only caught a giant shark, Merena pushed her way through her fellow pirates. A tear fell from her face as Merena glanced upon the nets. There in front of her lay a limp yellow-tailed mermaid. Bending down, Merena began to remove the nets that held the mergirl down.

"Don't worry, don't worry," was all Merena could bring herself to say as she brushed the mergirl's hair from her fear-stricken face. A pair of hands grabbed Merena by the shoulder and pulled her up.

"Why did you use a net? Where's the giant fishing hook?" chills raced down Merena's body as the voice of Queen Ramona echoed through the crashing waves, "You know I like the sight of a mermaid dangling from a hook better than a puny, old net." Memories rushed through her mind. The hook was the most painful thing she had ever experienced. She had promised herself that if she had to catch mermaids it would not be with that hook. Regaining her confidence, Merena glanced towards Adrie for guidance.

Adrie nodded and swung her sword, "Listen, we didn't feel like bringing the hook out," Merena gasped as Adrie sliced the net open with her sword and kicked the terrified mermaid, "Does it really matter though? We caught the mermaid, did we not?" Queen Ramona rolled her eyes and pulled a conch shell out of her pocket.

A sharp pain exploded against Merena's skin as Queen Ramona placed the shell into Merena's hand, "It's your turn. Make her belong to me!"

Merena felt paralyzed. Her body shook uncontrollably. Merena was unsure of what to do. She hadn't realized that she was going to have to bring true physical pain upon the poor mermaid. She knew this would surely traumatize the girl for life. Her pirate crew looked at her with laughter. Some of them even whispered thoughts of doubt. Merena even heard one ask if they could throw Merena overboard if she didn't have the strength to complete her job.

Taking a step forward, Merena watched as the pirate crew beckoned to her as they released the mermaid from her net, grabbing her arms to bind her down.

"Do it!" Queen Ramona commanded as she kicked Merena forward. Hesitant, Merena placed the shell into the mergirl's hand. Merena locked eyes with the mergirl and whispered, "I'm sorry."

A scream escaped Merena as the shell began to glow. Shaking in pain, Merena felt as if a thousand jellyfish were stinging her. The pain increased to an unbearable level, sending Merena crumbling to the ground. Still holding on to the mergirl's hand, Merena felt the shell begin to shrink. Holding on as long as she could, Merena watched as the girl was surrounded by the same light as she had been. An emptiness took hold of Merena as she watched the mergirl fall to the ground. Lost and confused, the mergirl stared at her long pale legs.

Merena was unsure if she could ever live with herself. She had taken this mergirl's world away, just as Queen Ramona had done to her.

Queen Ramona hit her staff to the ground, sending an electric shock across the waves. Glancing at her glowing hand, Merena felt herself slipping away.

Queen Ramona smiled, "Take this fish away. We will deal with her tomorrow." Turning towards her quarters, she glanced back at Merena, "Wonderful job today, Merena. I can't wait to see what else you can give me." For an instant, Merena felt a strange pride sweep over her, but it quickly retreated as she watched Queen Ramona's eyes, lit with an evil fire, as she walked away.

Exhausted, Merena fell to the ground, watching the mergirl she had imprisoned be carried below deck. The world began to slow. The waves crashed against her skin, but Merena didn't care. The wind stung her face, but Merena didn't notice. The pirates continued their duties, but Merena sat and watched the thunderous waves crash along the deck. Water splashed against her face, yet Merena did not flinch.

Adrie pulled Merena to her feet and guided her towards the captain's quarters. Merena felt the waves push *The Siphon* back and forth. But it did not seem to faze her. All she could see was Queen Ramona's eyes staring deep inside her. *BAM!* The Captain's Quarters door slammed shut, silencing everything.

"Merena what happened," Adrie, frustrated, sat Merena onto her bed, "I mean we've been training for two weeks now. I thought you were ready. You looked so weak and confused. You can't do that as a captain. That makes me ... us, look bad. Merena, are you even listening?"

Shaking her head, Merena whispered, "I don't know." She felt as if a piece of her had been taken. *But what?* It was as if her strength had been pulled out of her. Her confidence vanished. She felt weak. Her heart was longing for something.

Adrie looked down at Merena and sighed with irritation, "Get some rest and we will figure this out in the morning."

Adrie hesitantly looked back at Merena before leaving, "We will figure out what happened." And with that Merena was alone. She didn't even hear Adrie shut the door as her head hit the pillow. She tried with all her might to stay awake, to think, to figure out what was wrong with herself, but she couldn't. She felt herself slipping away. Her eyes were beginning to fall as she reached for a blanket. Merena tried to let her mind wander, but all she could see was the glow from Queen Ramona's eyes. The glow from Queen Ramona's staff. The glow that was consuming her mind. And then there was nothing.

CHAPTER TWELVE

Banished and Abandoned

Adelia's bad day tumbled into an even worse one. Sitting at a starfish table was Tiera's father and her two sisters. Adelia was unsure of what to say. *Should she tell them what had happened? Or wait for her mother to return? What would she say to them about being in their home?*

Tiera's father rose from his seat and swam with such authority that Adelia thought she would tremble at his feet. Backing up, Adelia felt his intimidating eyes stare down at her.

"Who are you?" his voice was like thunder echoing through the house.

Adelia looked to the ceiling as if searching for an answer. His glare made her want to admit to anything so she could leave his presence.

"Obviously, you are not from here. Speak up, why are you here?" he commanded. The two sisters had begun to swim closer to her, admiring her blue tail and dark hair.

"Father, how'd she make it this far without being caught?" one sister questioned.

He glared at her, angry at the lack of response from Adelia, "Speak now or I'll take you to the shell station myself. Officer Clamshell will be thrilled to have you behind bars!"

"Father," the identical twin touched her father's shoulder, "She's only a child." Adelia realized she was wasting time. Tiera could be miles away by now.

Taking a deep breath, Adelia let out a weak, "My name is Adelia. I … I need your help."

"I will not help someone from the *Fallen Sea Kingdom*. Do I look like a fool to you?" the man huffed. Taken aback, Adelia regained her posture. *Surely he would help his own daughter. Even if he threw Adelia out afterward.*

"It's about Tiera. She's been captured," Adelia began to speak a thousand words a minute, "She … we were swimming together near the surface, when all of a sudden a giant storm erupted and somehow we were separated. I searched for Tiera, but the next thing I knew she was in the net being lifted onto a pirate's ship. I am so, so sorry, but if we go now, I think we can save her." Adelia watched as the once strong man stumbled to the ground, devastated. The sisters touched his back, unable to speak.

"Get out!" the man screamed, "Get out of my home! Leave us to mourn the loss you have brought upon us. May you never return until my daughter is brought home!" Shocked, Adelia rushed toward the door, shaking, blood rushing through her veins. *Where should she go? What should she do?*

Bursting through the door, Adelia's vision was invaded by bright lights and mermaids and mermen swimming to the beat of the ocean. Adelia began to swim as fast as she could toward anywhere. Anywhere that would get her away from here.

Only slowing to make a turn or to not run into anyone. Fear engulfed her. *What if she were to be caught? Would she be killed?*

Making a sharp turn, Adelia rushed into a dark alleyway. A sharp pain in her tail sent her flying into a wall. Her head felt light and dizzy. Glancing up, she saw the face of her adopted mother.

"What…. Why…" Tiera's mother helped Adelia up.

Tears of glass began to fall from Adelia's face. She could feel them rub against her face, each a painful reminder that her best friend, her chosen sister, could be dead.

"She's been captured, Tiera, by pirates. We were playing near the surface when a storm blew in. We lost sight of each other," the words barely flowed out of Adelia's mouth, "I … I saw her in a net being lifted onto a boat! I swam as fast as I could, but then your husband and daughters saw me and threw me out. I didn't know what to do! Oh, Mom!" Tears were streaming down her face now.

Tiera's mother grabbed her hand and fought to hide the fear upon her face, "Adelia, we've got to get you out of here."

"But where will I go?" Adelia tried to find a glimpse of hope in her adopted mother's eyes. There was none.

"Tiera might as well be dead. We will have to get you through the city gates unseen," a tear fell from the mother's eyes and into her hand as she continued, "Follow me." Her adopted mother grasped her hand, pulling her through the water. Tears rushed down Adelia's face, blurring her vision of the passing buildings and confused by swimmers. After two sharp turns and one rushed stop, they made it to the city gates undetected.

Adelia's body shook violently as her adopted mother held her in her arms, "Once out of the city you will have to swim away from here. Find shelter, maybe return to your kingdom," Looking into Adelia's eyes, she sighed, "Maybe one day when you are older you can come find me again. I'd like to see you all grown up. I am going to miss you, but this is the way it must be. I am sorry … I wish I could have done something. You deserve so much better."

"You were more than good to me," Adelia whispered. A crowd of curious eyes had begun to gather behind the two.

Her adopted mother glanced behind them, "You have to go before they alert the guards. Who knows, someone may have already." Adelia lowered her head. *Was this the last time she'd ever get to say goodbye to her?*

"I love you, my daughter."

A chill raced down Adelia's spine. If she never found her real mother, it would be ok. At least she had a mother that loved her as if she was her child and that was more than enough for Adelia.

Determination burst through Adelia's veins as she locked eyes with her adopted mother, "I'll find them. I'll find my family and then I'll return. No matter the results, I'll search for Tiera. I promise." And then Adelia burst towards the surface, swimming as fast as she could, only glancing back once to see a hopeless mermaid staring at her.

❈

Evalyn held her conch shell close to her heart. She had been practicing extra hard the past week because she had overheard one of the dolphins say they were going to be performing in front of an actual crowd. A crowd of fish? Mermaids? Evalyn didn't know, but she was so sure that she would be picked for the solo that she could hardly hide her excitement.

"Attention fellow performers. I have exciting news!" spoke Zoe, a loud and controlling dolphin who usually stayed away from Evalyn, "We have gotten an amazing opportunity to perform on stage in the Western Sea Kingdom in front of thousands of mermaids!" Cheers erupted from the dolphins around Evalyn. She felt the excitement she had been holding in explode like a volcano as her smile continued to grow and grow. Evalyn 's cheer was interrupted when she felt a tap on her shoulder. It was Lulu.

"Are you as excited as I am?" Evalyn expressed, as she felt her body move to the celebratory music that had begun to fill the room. A look of disappointment lay on Lulu's face as she pulled Evalyn off into an empty room. Evalyn was confused. *How could Lulu be upset at a time like this?*

Hesitantly, Lulu seemed like she was searching for her words, "Evalyn… I'm sorry. I know how excited you must be about, um, this performance."

"I know! I have never performed in front of a crowd before. I am a little nervous," Evalyn glanced back toward the main room of the cave. It looked and sounded like a party had started.

"Um, right, you've never performed in front of a crowd because we were … are protecting you. We wouldn't do anything if we didn't think it was what's best for you. You understand that, right?" Lulu held Evalyn's gaze.

Evalyn nodded, "Of course I do. So, Lulu, what's this all about? I really…"

Before Evalyn could finish, Lulu blurted out, "You can't go! I'm so sorry but we don't think it would be safe," Evalyn's heart sank like a rock and tears were threatening to fall, "The Western Sea Kingdom and the Northern Sea Kingdom are not seeing eye to eye at the moment. They are almost … well, they are at the brink of war. They probably wouldn't even let us in if they knew you existed. Who knows, they could even take you away from us. We would never want that to happen."

Evalyn looked away from Lulu, "Are you going to stay with me?" was all Evalyn could manage. Lulu simply looked away, shaking her head no. *Why had they let her practice with the band if they had never intended for her to be a part of it? Was she even as good as they had told her?* A spark of anger began to roar in Evalyn.

"You are going to go? Leave me alone! Just ... just like my mother did? Who knows, maybe I won't be here when you get back!" Evalyn knew that hurt Lulu, by the look of disbelief that had flooded her face. Evalyn felt sorry the moment the words left her mouth, but she meant what she said. *Hadn't she?*

Lulu straightened up, "Listen here, you will be here when I get back! A few of us are staying behind, anyway. And if I hear even as much as a peep out of you, you will be sanded! Is that clear?" Evalyn nodded. She had never been sanded, but she had heard stories that you get to do nothing; stuck in your room with fear of dying of boredom.

"Yes, Lulu," Evalyn lowered her head in defeat.

But Lulu wasn't finished, "Listen, Evalyn, you are a great kid, but you sure are independent for your age. You're just a child. You need us. When you are sixteen, you may leave. You can do whatever you please with your life when you are not under our roof. Maybe I'll even help you find your Mom. But as of now, you will stay here and behave yourself."

Evalyn nodded. She had never seen Lulu look so angry and upset. She wished she could take back what she said. Evalyn felt like a thousand pounds were thrusted upon her shoulders as Lulu led her past the room where everyone was celebrating and to her sleeping quarters.

"It's late and we're all tired. Get some sleep and we will talk more tomorrow before I leave," Lulu started to head back to the party but turned and sighed, "You'll get to use your talent one day. You'll get to perform in front of millions upon millions. Just be patient." And then she left Evalyn with just her whirling thoughts. Thoughts that crashed in her mind like a tsunami sent to destroy her mind. One second she was angry, then she was sad. If anyone had seen her they would have watched a child crying herself to sleep, not knowing that this was how she got to sleep every night. Longing for a mother who would know how to comfort her during these confusing times.

Merena woke to the sound of a terrible banging. Glancing around she felt the ship swaying. *Had the ship stopped?* Head ringing, Merena slipped out of bed in her damp, dirty clothes from the night before. She was a sight. Her hair was severely matted and seaweed intertwined within her braids. Her body shivered as she quickly changed into an almost identical outfit. A large bang caused Merena to instinctively jump for cover behind the captain's desk.

Slowly rising, Merena ignored her hair for the time being and slipped on her boots. Slowly opening the door a crack, Merena blinked as a burst of light invaded her eyes. *What was that sound?* Glancing around, Merena saw that the boat had stopped. Most of the crew was gathered around the trapdoor, cheering at the top of their lungs. Forgetting about her current appearance, Merena wandered over to the group. Anger developed deep within her as she saw the truth of what they were doing. The pirates held sticks banging against the trap door where the captured mermaid lay.

"Stop! Stop taunting her!" Merena yelled as she shoved her way towards the pirates. The pirates looked at each other before bursting into laughter.

"You expect us to listen to someone who looks like they just got washed up on shore?" One pirate laughed.

Merena jumped onto a barrel and felt an unfamiliar confidence overtake her, "Silence! Will someone please tell me why we have stopped sailing because of this?" The pirates shrugged her off.

Stomping her right foot, Merena pointed to the top deck, "Go and do your duties or I, as captain, will have something done with you!" Merena felt her voice carry across the ship as the pirates' faces fell. Slowly the pirates dispersed. A smile came across Merena's face as she stepped down onto the deck. She suddenly wished Adrie had seen her. *Where was she anyway?*

A quick whimper filled Merena's ears as she opened the trapped door. Slowly descending the ladder into the dark room, Merena felt the burden of last night's events surface back up. She felt heavy, unsure what she would say to the fragile mergirl. Stepping onto the wooden floor, Merena turned slowly to face a broken mergirl curled up in a ball. Merena approached the mermaid slowly. Silently sinking down beside her, Merena watched the broken mergirl. Each cry that left the mergirl's mouth pierced Merena's heart. It was all she could do to keep from bursting into tears herself. She had done this to this poor mergirl.

"I'm sorry," Merena managed.

The mergirl lifted her head and turned to look directly at Merena, "You're sorry? You took me away from my family and you're sorry? You left my sister alone and helpless, but you're sorry?" the mergirl grabbed Merena's hand and pointed at the mark of Queen Ramona, "You did this to me!"

Merena felt a flood of tears burst down her face, "I had no choice. But please let me explain. I'm like you." The girl shook her head and lowered it back into her arms.

"I'm like you, but I won't let you live like I have for the past decade of my life. But without you, more of us will be captured and sent into a brutal servanthood," Merena begged, "Please give me a chance?"

The mergirl didn't move. Wondering if she should continue to speak, Merena searched her brain for what to say. Before she could think of anything more, tapping came from the top of the trap door. Looking up, Merena saw dark, tall pirate boots descending the ladder that led to the bottom of the cage. It was Adrie. In the dark, Adrie looked tired as she nodded for Merena to return to the main deck. Reluctantly following, Merena sighed, if only she had had more time. If only she had said more.

Merena began to speak to Adrie as they stepped on the deck, but Adrie shook her head no and walked towards the Captain's Quarters. Confusion had become a norm for Merena, so she followed in silence wondering if her life was going to change yet again.

Water pressed against her face as Adelia swam as fast as she could towards the surface. Fear fueled her. She was uncertain what would happen to her if she got caught by the merguards. *Would they kill her? Send her to the Northern Sea Kingdom?* Blocking thoughts of worry from her brain, Adelia decided her best option was to get as near to the surface as possible. She hoped that if she was being followed, they would become fearful of the surface and stop their pursuit.

The water became unsteady as she neared the surface. It pressed against her, pushing her this way and that. Not wanting to adventure out of the ocean, Adelia decided she would swim directly under where the water turned to the sky. It was a challenge. Every few seconds, she was flung up out of the water by giant waves. Not knowing where she was going or how she was going to survive, Adelia kept pressing forward, hoping to get as far away from the Western Sea Kingdom as possible.

Evalyn arose from the bed confused. *Why had she woken up?* Glancing around, Evalyn saw that even the glowing jellyfish were still asleep. Their light was dim, not allowing Evalyn to see much from her bed. At first, Evalyn thought it must have been nothing, but then there it was again. *Whispers?* Slipping out of her covers, Evalyn crept over to her cracked door. As her vision cleared, Evalyn's heart sank. All her dolphin friends were hurriedly packing for their trip, rushing this way and that. Just as Evalyn was about to slip back into bed, Lulu caught her attention. She was writing a long letter. Lulu, although she faced away from Evalyn, looked as if she was crying. Holding up the letter, Lulu nodded her head before placing it down. Slowly, she smoothed the letter out and then placed a shell down on the upper right corner. She turned and nodded to the other dolphins. Slowly each one left the cave. Evalyn felt her heart quicken. *What was happening? Why were they leaving?* She wanted with all her might to follow them out of the cave and into the deep blue sea, but something held her back. She wanted to move, to scream, to do something, but she couldn't. She stood there, heart pounding, as she watched her family leave her.

Evalyn's heart stopped. She felt as if she was going to pass out. The feeling in her tail went numb. Floating to the ground, all she could think was that she had been abandoned, yet again.

❧

Merena watched as Adrie pulled a large map out of her boot. *How did she hide it in there?* Merena decided she would never know all Adrie's tricks. The map rolled open upon Merena's desk nearly knocking over everything in its path. Stepping closer, Merena examined the map. It was unlike any she had ever seen. It was sectioned off into four regions, islands were labeled in faded cursive, while mysterious continent names were written in bold print on the outline of the map. It was marked up with freshly printed X's, stars, circles, and shells.

"What is this?" Merena touched the map. The rough texture felt extremely old.

Adrie nodded for Merena to sit, "I've been studying the legend of Klamp in great detail for the past couple of days. I've recorded my findings on this map. Do you understand it?"

Merena studied the map. *Shells, X's, Stars, Circles?* They meant nothing to her.

"Ok, let me explain. The Shells mean a mermaid was captured at this spot. Stars mean a mermaid was sighted," Merena's heartbeat quickened, "Circles mean treasure was found there and X's mean buried treasure."

Merena felt sick. Everywhere there was treasure found or assumed to be buried there were ten or more stars and shells.

"Do you see what I see?" Adrie questioned.

Merena nodded. The Northern Hemisphere Adrie had marked off was correct. She knew exactly where all four merkingdoms existed. The question was whether Adrie had connected the dots.

"I have marked off four sections. Each has its own area that has a cluster of mermaid sightings and buried treasure. But if you notice, the northern hemisphere has an extremely large amount of buried treasure and very few mermaid sightings, while the rest of the kingdoms have more mermaid capturings and found treasure."

Merena only nodded. *Where was she going with this?*

"This is where we are going," Adrie pointed across the outer northern lands. It was full of X's, "Can you imagine how rich we are going to be?"

"I don't want any treasure," Merena confessed.

Adrie laughed, "Don't say that in front of the boys. They'd take your word for it. A pirate lives for treasure. That's why all of us are here," Merena wondered if that was also why Adrie was so nice to her. She hoped not.

"Now listen, we are going to be venturing into the northern hemisphere in two days. I am hoping by then Queen Ramona will be gone and will have taken that mermaid below deck with her."

"Oh, I was thinking she could stay with us," Merena interrupted.

Adrie just stared at Merena for a moment, "Um, well, I guess. It's just that I don't want another incident like what happened the other night." Merena wanted to explain that it wasn't the mermaid's fault, but Queen Ramona's. She wanted to explain the feeling she gets when Queen Ramona seems to suck the life out of her. But for some reason, she couldn't. Her mind felt heavy as her memories seemed to blur. Her eyes felt frozen, locked in on the Northern Hemisphere. She gasped as her body seemed to go numb, but Adrie didn't even notice. Adrie just smiled and said, "I'll see you in a little while. Just study that map. I'll figure out what to do with Queen Ramona." *Had Merena said something to Adrie?* She didn't think she had. A chill swept across Merena's body as quickly as she felt normal again. Sitting down on the wooden desk, she stared at the map, wondering if her daughters were anywhere near where she was heading.

CHAPTER THIRTEEN

Tears of Crystal

E valyn reluctantly moved towards the note Lulu had left. The cave was silent. The water was still. Hope fled from Evalyn as she passed empty room after empty room. No one had stayed behind. The water seemed to grow heavier as if she was pushing a thousand pounds as she crept closer to the note. Evalyn's eyes connected with a small conch shell that laid beside the note. Grabbing the shell, she held it close to her heart, hoping it would bring her a little comfort. Glancing at the note, she could tell it was long and written in a hurry. *What had happened that caused them to flee so quickly?*

Grabbing the note, it felt soft and fragile in her hands. She let herself float to the ground as she read the beginning words, *"Dear Evalyn: our light and joy, a mysterious blessing, in a dark world."*

Adelia glanced back. Her previous home was nowhere in sight. All she could see was a dark blue, the color of her tail. The world above her was dark as well. Knowing she would be extremely hard to see, feelings of adventure and confidence replaced her previous feelings of loneliness and fear. Glancing down, Adelia made her way towards the sea floor, hoping to find the seaweed bed she had explored with Tiera. Adelia knew she should not have felt excited, because her best friend was trapped on a ship full of murderous pirates; however, this was the chance she had been waiting for. She no longer had anything holding her back from finding her Mom. And something was telling her that if she could find her Mom, she would find Tiera.

Unable to control the shaking that had swept across her body, Evalyn slowly read the letter.

"Dear Evalyn: our light and joy, a mysterious blessing in a dark world,"

I know this is very bad timing, but the day we have been fearing has occurred. The Western and Southern Sea Kingdoms have signed an alliance against the Northern Sea Kingdom. All dolphins have been called into service. Some of us will be musicians during the battle, some nurses, others will carry the injured upon our backs. It is only a short time before the Northern Sea Kingdom declares war upon them as well. However, there is something we have kept from you, the reason we never let you play music in public. The Northern Sea Kingdom used to be the kingdom that kept the sea balanced. They convinced the other kingdoms not to start a war. This all changed ten years ago, about the time we found you. The soon to be Queen and King disappeared the same night the reigning King and Queen were killed. It all was a blur and before anyone knew it, there was a new king sitting on the throne of the Northern Sea Kingdom. And he was … is brutal. He throws citizens into slavery without a second thought and uses magic to torture citizens who leave the borders of his kingdom. If you were found out he would surely kill you. Now that war is among us, nowhere is safe. We all dread the thought of you being captured by the Northern Sea King, but we also feel the Southern and Western Sea Kingdoms would use you as an example. We must serve our Queen and King. We no longer can keep you hidden; you must do this yourself. I prayed I'd be able to protect you until you were sixteen, but I guess ten years old will have to do. You are special in more ways than you or I know. By this note is a conch shell I was going to give you when you were sixteen. It was attached to your hair when I found you. Please, take it. Remember, I love you and when you're older and this war is over, come find us. I want to see the beautiful young lady you will become. Do not stay long in the cave, for the Southern and Western Sea Kingdoms are searching caves at this very moment. They will reach our cave by nightfall. Use your dark tail and hair to your advantage. Hide deep in the sea and no one will find you. I pray someone will come along and help you, but as of now I beg you to trust no one. You no longer know who is on your side. Remember, this is war that we are entering.

Yours truly,
Lulu and your adopted family.

Adelia fiddled with the shells in her hair as she sat in the seaweed bed where she had been found. It lay six miles away from her previous home, but she felt safe. Pulling a small conch shell out of her braids, she held it close. It was all she had from her past. Tiera had said that she had discovered it woven in her hair when she found her. Her fingers chilled as they moved over the smooth shell. It always amazed her how it had not begun to wear. The delegate shell was over a decade old, yet it looked new. In her hands lay the only clue she had to her long lost family. Maybe this was why she collected and studied conch shells. Ever since Adelia could remember, she had been determined to become an expert on them. To a stranger, she was an expert. Adelia could identify 98.5% of the shells with which she came in contact. By studying the creases and cracks that designed the shell, she could know what the shell had been through and where it was from. The shell in her hand, however, was a mystery. Not only did she not know where it was from, but she also couldn't figure out why it had not begun to wear. The answer seemed to pull at her heart. This shell seemed to break any logical knowledge that merscientists had written about in the hundreds of books she had studied. Adelia sat the shell upon the sand and studied it. According to Tiera, this was the last place the shell had settled before she had found it. *Where had the ocean taken it before it lay here attached to me?*

A gust of water pushed Adelia into the sand, tossing the conch shell North. Adelia's heart stopped as she grasped ahold of the shell and quickly wove it back into her hair. Glancing up, she realized that a school of fish were hurriedly making their way South. Turning back to the North, Adelia let her mind race. Tiera had said she was from the Northern Sea Kingdom. *Wouldn't that mean that's where her shell was from? Why was she wasting her time looking for a dark blue shell foreign to this region when her answers lay to the North. If she found where this shell was from, would she find her family?*

Staying hidden amongst the seaweed, Adelia slowly made her way upward until she was near the extremely large school of fish. Chills ran through her body as she saw the absolute fear in the fish's eyes. The fear to know why they were running pounded in her brain, but she knew that if she became aware of the danger, she would turn back from her mission. Staying still until the fish were nearly out of sight, Adelia felt the cool seaweed hit against her. Breaking away from her protected hiding place, Adelia burst through the sea. Determined not to look back, Adelia focused on the dark waters in front of her.

The ocean towards the North was known to be dark and mysterious, barely anyone traveled from or to the Northern Sea Kingdom. Today it seemed to Adelia that many were traveling away from it. In the past mile, Adelia had seen three schools of fish heading West, East, South, but none towards the North. As the waters began to settle into a darker blue, Adelia felt a sudden safety. A peace like none she had ever felt. It seemed to engulf her. The darkness of the waters had no effect on her. In fact, her eyesight seemed to have been enhanced. The brilliant area of blues that designed the coral along the seafloor amazed her. They had to be ten times brighter than the ones that had been in her previous home. Almost instantaneously, the peace faded into a sudden tiredness. Unsure of the time, nor the last time she had eaten, Adelia searched for somewhere to rest. She noticed a long line of indigo coral. Following the trail, Adelia watched as she neared the edges of each coral piece, they seemed to shine a brilliant light blue and then fade back to indigo as she passed. *How interesting.* Seconds later, Adelia let out a sigh of relief. Lying before her was the entrance to a cave, a cave full of the seemingly magical indigo coral. Not caring who she met inside, Adelia rushed into the cave. Noticing a soft section of coral just large enough for a bed, Adelia felt as if the cave was meant for her. Laying her head down, Adelia said a silent prayer before drifting off into a deep sleep.

Shaking, Evalyn watched as a crystal fell from her eyes, smashing into pieces against the heavy letter. Nothing made sense anymore. *Why had the kingdoms gone into war? Why did it matter if some king and queen had died?* All she wanted to do was get all dressed up with glitter and sparkles and play her conch shell upon a grand stage. *Was that selfish? Was wanting to chase after her dreams really that selfish?* She could see herself shining bright like the sun in front of millions. Yet, just as quickly as the dream had been born into her mind many years ago, it seemed to fade away, locking itself inside a large treasure chest of unanswered questions.

As she began to regain the feeling in her muscles, Evalyn focused on the current issue. She was homeless, friendless, and family-less. She had no one to turn to. Weaving the fragile conch shell into her hair, Evalyn swam towards the cave exit. Instead of seeing the usual colorful and vivid sea, Evalyn was met with a deep blue sea of great emptiness. It seemed to have been there all along hidden behind the love and joy. Swimming deeper into the sea, Evalyn decided she would travel North. Everywhere else she was unwanted and hated, there was no hope for her there. A large octopus spun up toward the world above, gracefully gliding past Evalyn. If it had been another day, Evalyn would have been amazed by its size. As the octopus continued on its journey, Evalyn wondered if he knew where he was going. *Or was he as lost as her?* A deep wound in her heart stabbed her with each pounding beat. *Would her mother be in the Northern Sea Kingdom? What about Father? Had he fallen along with the Northern Sea Kingdom? Or was he a part of the evil that had begun to grow in the hearts of the Northern people?* No, Evalyn refused to think like that. She knew her mother and father didn't give her up on purpose and she was sure that they were only waiting for her return. Letting out a sigh, Evalyn felt a feeling of confidence come from within her. She wasn't lost. She had someone waiting for her. All she had to do was find them.

CHAPTER FOURTEEN

Land

The wind blew against Merena's face as she watched the waters rush by below. The wind threatened to pull her over and into the depths of the sea. It was her favorite place to think lately. Each water droplet that pounded her face reminded her of each passing second. It seemed the longer she was under Queen Ramona's control the less likely she would return to the sea. Part of Merena begged her to jump over the rail and return home. Yet, Merena knew there would be no good that would come from that. She would either die or she would be diving deeper into Queen Ramona's magic.

Adrie had promised Merena that Queen Ramona would have returned to her royal throne by now. Nevertheless, two months had passed and Queen Ramona still stood upon the top deck looking as radiant as usual. Her large violet dress seemed to be six feet wide at the bottom and five inches at the waist. Queen Ramona smirked at the pirates below; they were basically her minions. Each wanted to prove themselves more worthy to their Queen. Because the closer you are to the Queen, the more respect and riches are likely to come knocking at your door.

Within two months, Merena and her crew had captured four mermaids, all from the Eastern Sea Kingdom. Each capture had sent Merena into the same situation as the first. Due to her wanting to talk with the other mermaids, Merena had been banned from having any encounters with anyone below deck. No matter how hard Merena tried, she couldn't shake the feeling that Queen Ramona's glaring eyes were burning a hole straight through her. A scream interrupted Merena's thoughts. It was Queen Ramona.

"Land! I see land!" Queen Ramona pounded down the stairs to the main deck, nearly knocking a pirate into the sea as she went. The pirates let out a cheer of delight and began barking out orders.

"Scan the island. Look for any inhabitants," One yelled as Adrie nearly hit Queen Ramona with a trap door.

"Watch where you are standing, your Majesty," Adrie scuffed as she rushed over to Merena, "Here's our first stop. Are you ready?"

Merena shook her head. This was all Adrie had talked about for the past three days. It was their first stop on her secret treasure hunt. *What was Adrie expecting her to do when she found this so-called mermaid enchanted treasure?*

"Don't get nervous on me now!" Adrie lightly shoved Merena into the side of the ship, "We are going to uncover some of the most famous treasures to be hidden! We are going to be rich! Don't you understand?"

"Yeah, but what about Queen Ramona?" Merena still wasn't stoked about this treasure hunting thing.

"Oh, her? The boys will handle her and maybe will catch another mermaid to keep her company. She really enjoyed the last one we caught, but she is getting a little testy," Adrie motioned for Merena to follow her, "You wouldn't happen to know where any Northern Mermaids reside around here, would ya?"

"Um ..." a loud chorus of laughter burst from behind Merena.

"You are hilarious, but I must change into my exploring clothes. James and Jaxson come on," James and Jaxson nearly stumbled over each other as they fought to grab the door for Queen Ramona. Ignoring the scene, Adrie reached for the Captain's Quarter's doorknob. Just as her fingertips came in contact with the door, the oh so familiar voice pierced Merena's ears.

"Oh, Merena!" Queen Ramona stomped her foot upon the great deck, "I would like to see you in my room before we depart this great vessel and onto that mysterious island."

Almost instantaneously, Merena's body followed Queen Ramona's command. Merena felt as if something was dragging her forward as she nearly stumbled into the back of Queen Ramona's overly-sized dress. Merena wished she could turn back and ask Adrie to join her, but her body seemed drawn to Queen Ramona. As Merena entered Queen Ramona's Quarters, directly across from her own, she nearly gasped. It was at least triple the size of her own. Vines of thorns seemed to encircle the entire room; up and down a spiral staircase that led to what Merena thought was a library. *A library? Why in the deep blue sea would Queen Ramona need a library on a boat? What if they crashed? All those books ... ruined!*

"Please sit," Queen Ramona motioned for Merena to take a seat by a magnificent fireplace. *A fireplace? On a boat made of wood? What was this woman thinking?* Sitting down on what seemed like a one thousand dollar chair, Merena nearly jumped in surprise when she noticed James and Jaxson sitting on each side of her.

Jaxson leaned in towards Merena and grinned, "Hi Merena, it's been a while," Merena rolled her eyes, these guys were nuts.

"It's magic," James mentioned as he nodded toward the fireplace, "It won't set the boat on fire."

"Silence!" Queen Ramona commanded as she gracefully sat across from her three subjects, sceptre in hand, "Merena, I am disappointed. Do you happen to know why?"

Merena simply shook her head no. She knew Queen Ramona was about to tell her everything she had done wrong in the past year.

"Well, you see, we have been on this boat for what seems like five billion years. Quite ridiculous, if I do say so myself. Yet, we have only captured ... added five or six new servants," Queen Ramona rubbed the top of her sceptre causing it to glow. To Merena, it was enchanting how the top of the sceptre seemed to fade in and out of different shades of purple.

"I was hoping to find another mermaid as beautiful as you, yet we haven't seemed to have done that yet," Merena felt sudden guilt overtake her. *Why had she let her queen down?* Merena shook the feeling away. This was not her queen. Merena stared at the conch shell within the sceptre. All she wanted to do was feel it, be with it. It was almost as if it could replace everything that had been stolen from her. Like it could fill up the empty vases within her.

"Queen Ramona?" Merena stood up, "Why did you design a conch shell to be within your sceptre?" Aching with temptation, Merena took a step towards Queen Ramona.

A grinning Queen Ramona watched Merena, "Ah, I see you noticed. I did not put the conch shell within that pearl. I found this pearl on a voyage North once. Would you like to hold it?" Nodding her head, Merena grasped the top of the sceptre with her hand. A familiar pain struck Merena's bones, crumbling her to the ground, sceptre in hand. A purple cloud engulfed her causing Merena to relax as she felt herself floating in water. Opening her eyes, Merena could see what seemed to be a deep ocean coral reef. Swimming towards the brilliant blue coral, Merena watched as they seemed to glow as she approached, just like the ones she had played with as a kid. Swimming farther North, Merena nearly jumped in excitement when she realized this was her childhood playground. Nearly twenty feet stood between Merena and her favorite hiding place: a giant coral-infested cave. This is where she would come when she needed to think or simply to get away. Swimming deeper into the cave, Merena came to a section of the coral that was softer. Sitting, she looked down expecting to see her tail. Instead, a cry threatened to burst from within her. She still had legs. *This isn't real.*

Touching the coral beside her, Merena pushed back a piece that uncovered her childhood conch shell collection. Glancing at the three empty spots, Merena realized why she was here. She pulled a dark blue conch shell out of her hair and watched as a crystal fell from her eyes.

"Mom ... I'm sorry," was all she could say as her tears began to flow out of her.

As the purple mist that had settled around her began to resurface, Merena buried her head into her arms. The mist transformed into a large purple cloud and surrounded the weakened Merena, carrying her towards the surface. Pressure began to pound against Merena's chest as the air in her lungs began to disappear. Desperate, Merena struggled to swim towards the surface, before she passed out. Reaching her arms out into the mist, Merena touched the surface of the water.

Instantaneously, Merena opened her eyes to see an impatient Queen Ramona. Glancing at her hands, Merena nearly gasped to see that the sceptre had turned a deep blue, almost the color of her previously beloved tail.

"I'll take that," as Queen Ramona snatched the sceptre, Merena felt as if a part of her was being ripped away. Wishing to just touch the sceptre again, Merena tried to sit up. Her body was heavy and weighing her towards the ground. Merena stared at her hands, she was soaking wet. Glancing up she met eyes with a smirking Queen Ramona.

"You will bring me others like you, Merena," Queen Ramona barely said above a whisper, "You want to make your Queen happy, correct?"

Merena wanted so badly to say no, but part of her seemed to lean towards yes. *Why after all these years had she suddenly wanted to follow Queen Ramona?* She didn't understand.

"I will try," she managed as her mind suddenly turned to Adrie. *What if Queen Ramona discovers what we are up to? Would Queen Ramona simply take all the treasure for herself? Adrie would be so upset.... Yet again, what if this so-called unfindable treasure was meant to be kept hidden?*

Mind racing, Merena barely noticed that James and Jaxson had answered a knock at Queen Ramona's door. Glancing back, Merena was surprised to see Adrie stepping on one of James' shoes and shoving her way through the door. Adrie pushed her way to the clearly frustrated Queen Ramona.

James and Jaxson fell on their knees as they gasped, "We are so sorry. She shoved her way in." Adrie was now "patiently" waiting beside Queen Ramona who was clearly enjoying the attention from her servants.

"It is fine. James and Jaxson, see to it that my handmaiden has prepared my pre-exploration bubble bath and adventure outfit," Queen Ramona nodded for Adrie to take a seat, as James and Jaxson scurried away. Adrie boldly stayed standing and gave Merena an eyebrow raise. Merena glanced down. She was a sight. Her hair was messy and drenched, seaweed was all over her, and she was lying in a puddle of water on the floor. Quickly standing up, Merena pulled her hair out of her face as she joined Adrie in front of Queen Ramona.

"Well, what are we waiting for? You are the one who barged your way into my quarters, correct?" Queen Ramona tapped her foot and glanced at her perfectly painted purple nails.

Adrie shifted her feet, "Correct. Sorry if I put on a little show back there. Those two get on my nerves." Adrie was waiting for a response, but Queen Ramona had turned her attention to fixing her hair in a hand mirror.

"Anyway," Adrie continued, "We have decided to anchor here and row our way to shore and explore. We think it would be best to leave half the crew on board, due to the fact that there have been mermaid sightings in this area, according to Merena, of course."

Queen Ramona stood and walked towards the great fireplace, "Do you promise you will catch some ... unique mermaids for me?"

"Yes, that is always our goal," Merena almost giggled as Adrie rolled her eyes behind the back of Queen Ramona, "I believe we should split the rest of the pirates who are not staying on the boat into two groups. That way we can cover more ground. May I ask what your goal for this exploration is?"

Queen Ramona dramatically turned around, "Can a girl not want a little adventure every once and awhile?" Merena glanced at James and Jaxson who seemed to be gathering everything imaginable for a camp out. Bug spray, rain boots, nut mix ... you name it, they were stuffing it into a giant purple bag.

"If I enjoy this land enough, I may add it to my kingdom," A chill ran down Merena's back. If humans inhabited this land, then the mermaids would have to relocate. Would this all be Merena's fault?

"Very well then, your Majesty. I will prepare the pirate crews and assign the very best to you. Now, if you will excuse Merena and I, we too must prepare for departure," Adrie quickly turned and grabbed Merena's now shaking hand. Merena felt as if she was going to crumble to the ground as Queen Ramona nodded them on.

"I wish to leave in forty-five minutes," Queen Ramona called out.

"Of course, your Majesty," Adrie responded as she pushed Merena out the door and onto the main deck. Wobbling over to the side of the boat, Merena felt the terrible and all too familiar queasy feeling. Barely reaching the rail of the boat, Merena heard the groans of the pirates behind her. She felt Adrie's hand on her back, patiently waiting to remove Merena from the scene.

"Let's get you into some fresh clothes," Adrie whispered as she thrust her arms around Merena in order to carry her away from the mess she had left. Lightheaded, Merena grabbed the pain in her stomach. *When was the last time I ate?* Ever since her world had fallen apart, she had to remind herself to eat. Sometimes when she ate guilt consumed her. *What if her daughters lacked food to eat?* She did not deserve any of this. Merena reached for her bed and laid down, wishing for her thoughts to subside.

"Here," Adrie tossed an apple onto the bed beside Merena, "eat that." Adrie quickly shoved all her maps and notes into a large carry bag. She then packed enough apples and nuts to last Merena for two sunsets. Merena bit into the large juicy apple. This wasn't selfish. *How was she supposed to take care of her daughters if she didn't take care of herself?* Sitting up, Merena noticed a set of clothes laid out on the foot of her bed.

"Those are yours, "Adrie exclaimed without looking up from her task, "Hurry and get ready, so we can leave before everyone else. I've made it clear that I am heading out first to scout for danger. "

Throwing her bag over her shoulder, Adrie headed for the door, "Meet me out here in ten minutes. I'll have the rest of the crew in their groups by then."

Ten Minutes Later

Merena blocked the sun from her eyes as she ventured to the edge of the boat. She watched as Adrie barked orders, sending pirates this way and that. A chill ran through Merena's bones as she glanced towards Queen Ramona's door. Part of her feared what Queen Ramona would do if she found out about Adrie's separate plan. What scared Merena most was that Queen Ramona was not part of Adrie's original plan. Ramona was supposed to be gone. Every ounce of Merena longed to be separated from Ramona. But who was she kidding? Ramona would never leave her alone as long as she bore the mark. Holding her hand, Merena realized she was shaking. She needed to focus. She was about to embark on an adventure like no other. Merena could feel a slight excitement building inside her. This would be a day full of firsts. The first time she would get to touch a tree or climb upon a mountain. Leaning over the edge of the boat, Merena's hair danced with the wind. The air felt crisp against her face as she let out a deep breath.

"Alright, let's head down," Adrie nodded for Merena to follow behind her as she jumped over the side of the boat and into a smaller wooden boat. Shaking, Merena lifted herself up on the side of the boat and glanced down at Adrie.

"Jump," Adrie shouted.

Heart racing, eyes closed, Merena let her body fall into the lowering lifeboat with a thud. Glancing down, she rubbed her now extremely scratched knees.

"Pick a different boat!" Adrie yelled at a pirate who had swung his leg over the boat, "This one's occupied!" Water hit Merena's face as Adrie swung the large wooden oars into the water. To Merena, the water seemed to be restless. She sensed a heavy burden upon the water that seemed to be feeding the fear hidden within her.

"Are you sure about this?" Merena hollered above the waves.

"Of course. Look! Queen Ramona hasn't even gotten off *The Siphon*!" Adrie screamed. Glancing back, Merena nearly laughed. Queen Ramona was struggling to push herself over the edge of the boat. It was clear that Adrie and Merena would have a good hour before Queen Ramona would even start her journey into the uncharted land. Taking a deep breath, Merena let the sea run through her fingers. It was like someone holding her hand before something terrifying happens. Glancing at the sea, she nodded and thought, *it's all going to be ok.*

CHAPTER FIFTEEN

A Magical Encounter

Adelia woke with a start. Her body ached as she glanced around. Looking up, she realized she had fallen off her makeshift bed and onto the hard sea floor. No wonder her neck felt as if there was a giant knot in it. Rubbing her sore neck, Adelia followed the gorgeous coral back out of the cave to get a sense of her surroundings. Wondrous scenery filled Adelia's vision. Although the deep sea was naturally dark, the glowing coral painted a magnificent picture of wonder. Some of the coral stood over twelve feet tall, while others were as small as a button. Each had such detailed designs that would take hours to recreate. Searching her memory for anything that she might have read concerning such a place, Adelia picked up one of the shells that rested below her. The shell spiraled around itself with tiny diamonds imprinted upon its surface. Braiding the tiny shell into her hair, Adelia felt at peace. She wasn't afraid of the idea that she was alone in foreign waters, although she wasn't longing to go much further, knowing that she would be entering the Northern Sea Kingdom soon. Adelia glanced back at the cave that had become a makeshift inn.

"I'll stay one more night and then advance north. I don't think I'll find many answers here," Adelia confirmed to herself. Adelia's eyes widened as she watched the coral begin to match the pitch of her voice with vibrant colors Unknowingly, Adelia began to hum as she searched for more intriguing shells. The coral around her followed her lead, becoming brighter when she raised her voice and duller as she lowered. It was almost as if the coral was trying to sing along.

⋙⋘

Passion burned through Evalyn's veins as she pressed on. Evalyn had been swimming for over twenty-four hours but didn't feel any sense of fatigue. Was it the fear of the unknown or was it a sudden bravery keeping her going? Evalyn wasn't sure. The cool water flowed past her face as she continued on. For almost two hours, she had seen very few creatures traveling from the north. In fact, she had only seen a giant stingray and an old looking shark who both just wanted to mind their own business. Part of Evalyn longed to rest and sleep, yet something deep within her kept her pushing on. She was certain that there was a safe place for her to reside for a couple of days and the bottom of the sea floor wasn't it.

Up ahead, a large rocky mountain came into view. Slowing her pace, Evalyn examined the dark openings that led to the core of the mountain. Could this be the place she had been waiting to find? Pulse quickening, Evalyn approached one of the large holes and listened. A deep breath filled her ears. Backing away slowly, Evalyn tried another hole. Nothing. However, an uneasy feeling filled her stomach, so Evalyn turned away almost instantly. Swimming lower, Evalyn caught sight of a larger hole that seemed to resemble a doorway. Entering slightly, Evalyn slowed her heartbeat and let her ears listen to the soundwaves that seemed to almost bounce off the walls of the rocky cave. A beautiful sound comforted Evalyn's ears. It sounded almost like humming or maybe even a mother's lullaby. Inching deeper into the cave, Evalyn followed the sound. An eagerness overcame her. That sound seemed so familiar. *La la la … La la laaa … la la la la la…* Rushing now, Evalyn feared she would lose whoever was making the sound. She turned down one hallway after another until she reached an open room full of beautifully glowing coral. Glancing around, Evalyn noticed a softer portion of the coral where a box of shells lay. To Evalyn it seemed to be missing a couple of shells, but she would have to investigate that later.

Following the coral out of the cave, Evalyn listened for the humming. It had stopped. A gasp escaped her mouth as the outside world came into her vision. It was gorgeous, unlike anything she had seen before. There had to be millions of coral all around. *La La … La la la la….* There it was again. Where was it coming from? *Laaaaaaaa…*

Nearly hitting the top of the cave entrance in shock, Evalyn watched as the coral was reacting to the sound as well. Its color seemed to change as the song continued. An idea entered Evalyn's mind. *If I wait inside the coral cave … maybe the mysterious singer will appear.* Turning, Evalyn took one more look around until she gathered all her patience and returned to the cave.

❈

A shadow caught Adelia's eye near the entrance to the cave. Heart pounding, Adelia hid herself from the view of the cave. *Could someone have been watching her?* Peeking out, Adelia's heart raced like an hourglass almost out of time.

"No one could be in the cave," Adelia assured herself, "It was just the coral moving in the water…" Gathering herself, Adelia swam past the large coral near the side of the rocks that built the wall of the cave. *Was the cave really that scary looking earlier?* The corals no longer seemed to be the beautiful focal point of the cave. Now all Adelia saw were long dark shadows that crept along the cave floor. Peeking deeper into the coral lit cave entrance, Adelia saw nothing out of the ordinary. Slowly, she made her way back to where she had slept the night before. Sitting on the soft coral spot, Adelia picked up the mysterious coral box that had been left behind by someone. *Had that someone just returned for their shells?* Adelia hoped not. Not only was she not looking for any trouble, but she also kinda liked having a box for her shells. Unbraiding the shells she had found that day from her hair, Adelia began to hum once again. *La La La La…* The music pressed through her lips like a painful memory she had forgotten. Unsure of where she had heard the song or why it brought her comfort when she was alone, Adelia listened to her tone. *La La La La…*

Bang! A giant rock fell near the left side of Adelia, sending smaller rocks flying in every direction. Jumping back and away from the collision, Adelia covered her eyes as dust exploded into the air. It filled her lungs quicker than she could take a breath. Struggling to escape the tumbling cave, Adelia prayed a slight prayer. Adelia pressed forward, fighting to keep from panicking. All she had to do was get out of the cave. Rocks rubbed against her skin making marks and scratches. The water seemed to help Adelia escape as she made one last effort before bursting into the wide open sea. Fresh, dust-free water slammed against her face. Arms out wide, Adelia spun in a circle of triumph. Relief flooded through her body.

Turning around, Adelia gasped. The cave was destroyed. The once beautiful coral entrance was now a pile of rocks and dead coral. Their light had gone out. Swimming slowly towards the wreckage, Adelia looked around. *Did she do this?*

Or was someone else really out there? Adelia's heart quickened as she picked up a piece of broken coral.

Adelia nearly froze as a piece of the wreckage began to move slightly. *Was something under the rocks?* Unsure whether to run or help whoever was trapped, Adelia watched the rocks. Reaching for her heart, Adelia took a deep breath to steady her heart. Her breath seemed to be slipping away from her as she felt herself stop breathing. The rocks continued to crumble and move as a bluefin peeked from the surface. Seconds passed as Adelia watched the struggling tail continue to escape from the suffocating rocks. *Should she help whoever or whatever this was?*

A thousand pounds pressed against Evalyn's chest. Darkness invaded her as she struggled to remove the rocks that piled on top of her. Rocks invaded her short breaths as a pain struck her body. It flowed from the bottom of her tail to the center of her heart.

All at once, her physical presence seemed to be slipping away. Her head pounded as her mind began to wander. Rocks sliced and cut into her as her body pulled forward. *Was it just her or did feel like she was moving upward towards the surface?* Within seconds, Evalyn saw a burst of light. Trying to help the mysterious puller, Evalyn reached upward, but failed. All her strength had escaped. Dropping her head back into the rocks, Evalyn let the force drag her upward. Just as it felt like she was almost free, her eyes shut and she drifted off into a deep unconsciousness.

Pulling with all her strength, Adelia watched as a young mermaid surfaced from the bottom of the rocks. Fear swept over Adelia as the young mermaid's head violently fell back against the pile of rocks. Adelia winced at the sight. Blood, scratches, and deep sea rock dust covered the poor mermaids' bodies. Unsure what to do, Adelia grasped the young mermaid in her arms. She couldn't tell where she was from because of the dust that covered her body. Looking around, Adelia felt a sudden strike of worry. She had nowhere to go and nothing to help the injured mergirl.

As if it was an answer to a silent prayer, Adelia noticed the glowing coral again. She had once read that if you drop the juice from coral upon an open wound it would heal it. Gathering herself, Adelia swam over to the brightest coral. Grasping it within her hands, a sudden sense of peace flowed through Adelia. A surge of energy quickly followed as the coral easily popped from the seafloor.

Amazing! Adelia thought as she studied the large coral piece. Even though she had broken it from its roots, the coral still continued to glow as she carried it back to the mysterious mermaid. Glancing around, Adelia noticed that the waters past the magical corals seemed extremely lifeless. Not a creature was in sight, just a neverending sight of forbidding dark blue waters. She rested beside the injured mergirl and wondered, *would she come with me into the darkness? Or will my journey to the Northern Sea Kingdom continue to be alone?* Unbraiding the sharpest shell from her hair, Adelia studied the coral piece from the center.

"There," Adelia exclaimed as she pressed the sharp shell deep into the chest of the coral. A blue liquid oozed out of the coral. Adelia winced at its icy, slimy texture rushing all over her hands. A gasp escaped Adelia as the liquid seemed to absorb into her hands. All at once a power like a gust of wind hit Adelia exploding her hair into the same glowing blue as the coral. Dropping the coral piece, Adelia tried to fight the powerful force as it flowed through her. Within seconds her tail, too, began to burst into a monochromatic set of blues. *What was happening?*

The blue liquid oozed out of the coral onto the pile of crumbled rocks, and made its way to the powerless mermaid. Adelia felt almost unconscious, as if she were in another realm. Adelia screamed as her body gave into the power that seemed to be erupting inside her.

The coral liquid touched the unconscious mermaid and began to absorb into her, covering every wound and scratch on her body. The dust washed away as her body lifted, revealing her beautiful skin. The two mermaids' hair flowed towards the surface of the sea as they glowed a deep sea blue. Rotating around each other, the mermaids looked identical. Their tails sparkled a marvelous blue. Their hearts pounded to the sound of the sea. Deep sea coral miles away vibrated to that same beat as the waters began to spin. Swarming the mergirls, the water pushed them closer together. The force of their bodies collapsing into each other sent a wave of water in all directions. The power of the wave flattened homes, uprooted coral, and separated families of fish. The mergirls, however, were seemingly unaffected as they floated to the bottom of the sea floor.

CHAPTER SIXTEEN

Merena...

A surge of kinetic energy sent Merena and Adrie flying out of the lifeboat and onto the rough island sand. Merena grabbed her side as an unfamiliar stinging crept up it. Merena gasped as her body burst into a glow of vibrating blues. Her body felt as if it were on fire. Her eyes shone like a crystal as powerful magic surged through her. There was something familiar about it, as if the emptiness inside her was being refilled. A large wave splashed against Merena, tossing her back toward the sea. Her hands shook violently as the ocean seemed to grab her, pulling her deeper into the water. Merena gave in and let the water rush through her veins. The waves crashed into her, yet she didn't fall. No, it was like she was absorbing the power of the sea. For the first time since her capture, Merena felt as if she could escape and never look back. The ocean seemed to get deeper. It was as if she was being summoned into a never-ending hole. Each stroke of her hand felt like unexplainable power that she deserved.

"What was that? I have never had a wave throw me one hundred yards before!" Adrie's voice woke Merena like an alarm clock does to a good dream. Exaggerating, Adrie pulled herself up and began dusting sand off her clothing. Merena glanced at her hands. They were shaking uncontrollably. Pulling her violently shaking hands to her side, Merena walked ashore.

That was no ordinary wave, Merena thought. To Merena, that wave was different, almost magical. An unexpected sense of relief smashed upon Merena as she reflected back on the surge of energy. *Maybe it was a sign to continue on or to hurry?* Merena's eyes sparkled with something not from the human world, but from within Merena. *I haven't felt this free in years. What was the source of the magic?* It didn't feel evil to Merena. In fact, it felt like quite the opposite of that.

Glancing back at the sea, Merena laughed. Queen Ramona, soaking wet, was struggling to make it back on *The Siphon*. *At least that will give us some time.*

"Let's go," Adrie said as she grabbed their stuff, "We need to make it to the center of the island before nightfall, according to the legend."

"Why?" Merena asked as she grabbed the map from the pack on Adrie's side. Merena looked at the terrain that they would be covering, lots and lots of forest land until they reached a large mountain.

"So, you didn't study the map?" Adrie said as she began walking towards the wall of massive trees. Merena felt her cheeks turn red. She had studied it, but it was not like she had it memorized. Nor did she know what to expect. She hadn't ever walked on grass or even seen a wild land animal before.

Placing the map back in the pack, Merena confessed, "I did. Just not as much as you."

"I know, now let's pick it up a step," Adrie pushed forward as she hopped over a weathered, fallen tree. It all amazed Merena. The world outside of Queen Ramona's castle wasn't all that bad. It wasn't as pretty as a glowing underwater coral reef, but it was still pleasant, peaceful almost.

Merena and Adrie continued to climb over fallen trees, pass through shallow rivers, and piles of rock for three hours straight without rest. To Merena, it was the longest she had walked in her whole life. Sure, she could swim from the Northern Sea Kingdom to the Southern Sea Kingdom in less than two hours, but walking it? That would surely take her at least three days. Her feet begged her to sit and never stand up again.

Merena's heart skipped a beat as her foot got caught between two roots sending her face planting into a pile of mud. This had to be her least favorite part about being a human. Getting nasty. Underwater, there was no such thing, because there was a constant flow of fresh waters. You were never in the same waters more than once.

Mud stained Merena's face and all she wanted was to jump into the lake they had passed moments early. If only she could find a waterfall.

"You good?" Adrie was impatiently staring at Merena. Quickly jumping to her feet, Merena wondered how long she had been lying on the ground. It could have been five hours and Merena wouldn't have noticed.

"Listen we're getting close to the center, see?" Adrie had pulled out the map, "We've already passed these three rivers and this giant oak tree. We've only got about this much to go."

Merena looked at the distance Adrie measured out. About one seahorse and they had already gone about three seahorses.

"We've got this. Here, have a pear," Adrie pulled a large green fruit from a prosperous tree.

Merena reluctantly took the odd-looking fruit and slowly brought it up to her mouth. A glorious taste exploded upon her taste buds, flavor like nothing Merena had experienced before.

"Why have I never tried one of these?" Merena exclaimed as juice dripped down her chin.

"You did live underwater for half your life," Adrie laughed as she munched on a pear as well, "So, while we march on tell me, did you have fruit and greens and meat under the sea?"

Merena smiled, "Well, we had lots of greens like you. I can make a mean Hijiki Wrap. You use the seaweed found near the southern shell caves. Add in some mashed Agar and Dulse as the center and it's delicious."

Adrie made a face, "That sounds gross. What's Agar and Dulse?"

Merena let out a laugh, "It's a bit different. Agar is sweeter and has the texture of what you call jello. Dulse is saltier and a bit tougher, so they mix very well. They make a jelly-like spread that goes right on the Hijiki seaweed wrap. It's extremely great for your skin. I've been wanting some of it so bad lately. I guess my skin has gotten kinda rough, dry, and lacking nutrients since I left the sea."

"I've wondered why mermaids always seem to have perfectly glowing skin," Adrie threw the stem of her pear over a huge rock, "If you eat weird stuff like that, I guess you deserve it." Merena laughed as Adrie began making her way up a towering rock. Adrie easily scrambled to the top. *Why couldn't it be as easy as it looked?*

"Look at that! I can see the mountain," Adrie yelled as she stood on the rock, "We are only about an hour away." Merena's spirit dropped as quickly as it had risen. *Another hour?* She had to be kidding. Gripping till her hand turned as pale as snow, Merena made her way up the rock. Every bone in her body begged her to come back down, yet Merena knew that if she fell she wouldn't get back up and Adrie would have to carry her the rest of the way. Muscles burnt out, Merena swung her legs over the side of the rock where Adrie had previously been standing.

"Isn't it beautiful?" Adrie asked as she watched Merena from the ground below. Adrie was right. It was beautiful. A towering mountain expanding miles wide and nearly touching the heavens with its snow-kissed point. What looked like miles and miles of flowers led the way to the center of the mountain. Sliding down, Merena felt the rough rock scrape through her clothes and into her skin.

"Ouch," Adrie said as Merena felt the scrape that now had blood rushing out of it.

"I'm fine," Merena winced, "It's just a little scratch."

Merena watched amazed as Adrie grabbed a handful of flowers and began braiding them into a wrap. In the blink of an eye, the flowers transformed into a wrap long enough to go around Merena's wound on her leg. She then placed pressure on the wound, sending a minor pain through Merena's upper thigh. Biting her lip, Merena closed her eyes as Adrie wrapped the wound.

"There," Adrie said as she slapped her hands together, "Let's keep moving!"

Merena pushed the pain of the scrape to the back of her mind. It was only a nuisance. Pushing a large leaf out of the way, Merena followed Adrie deeper into the island, unsure of what she was going to find at the end of the journey.

❈

One Hour Later

A strange feeling grew inside Merena with each step she made towards the great mountain. Uncertain of where Adrie was taking her, Merena was no longer fearful, nor curious, but aware. Absent from the world around her, Merena watched a droplet of water fall from a great tree. Reaching her hand out, the droplet splashed upon her skin. She wanted to join the droplet as it would soon collide with the underground rivers that traveled through the center of the island. She knew that each droplet was making its own journey back to the ocean. Just like she was. The only difference was that the waters were guaranteed to return to the sea. Merena's journey was up to her.

An urgent feeling pulled Merena closer to the mountain's walls. Something was calling her deeper into the island. She was still sure Adrie was with her, however her present state didn't allow her to draw the strength to speak. Her body moved forward towards a dark, rocky hole in the side of the mountain. In the back of her mind, Merena felt as if someone was chanting her name. *Merena... Merena...*

"Merena!" Adrie grabbed the back of Merena's shoulder, throwing her back into reality, "Where are you going?"

Merena looked around. A long, rocky hallway faced Merena. Why had she been going this way?

"Um..."Merena's thoughts were all jumbly. *Merena...* Nearly knocking Adrie over in fright, Merena looked deep into the cave.

"Didn't you... I..." Confusion rushed through Merena's mind, "You don't hear that?" The look on Adrie's face answered that question. *Was she going crazy? Hadn't she heard someone calling her name?*

Merena... "There... That! Can't you hear it?" Merena walked deeper into the cave. She was certain someone or something was summoning her.

"Merena, listen. This is a dead end. There's nothing down here," Annoyance filled Adrie's voice, "Please, let's turn back."

"Just a little further," Merena replied. The voice seemed to be increasing in volume as they ventured deeper into the cave.

"Look!" Increasing her pace, Merena's eyes focused on a bright light up ahead.

Adrie finally seemed to commit to the adventure as her eyes too, saw the light, "What is it?" As the two girls came closer to the light, the cave walls began to narrow until there was barely enough space for them to slide through.

Merena... "I've got to get to that light," Merena felt a sense of urgency overcome her as she squeezed through the narrow space toward the light.

Adrie had stopped about ten feet back, "Merena... I'm staying back here. Ok?"

"Yeah, yeah. That's fine," Merena wasn't truly listening anymore. Her mind was transfixed on the emitting light. To Merena, it reminded her of a night light coral from the depths of the sea. Within a foot of the light, Merena was stopped by the narrowness of the rock-like walls of the cave. Without a second thought, Merena reached out and grabbed the light. A piercing cold round object filled her hands. *Merena... Merena... Merena...* The chants had turned into screams now. All Merena wanted to do was back away, yet she glued to the icy object. Fear arose from within her. *Pull, Merena, Pull...* Gripping hard, Merena used every ounce of strength from within her and pulled. The round object released its grip on the wall, nearly sending Merena flying backwards. Before Merena hit the ground, the walls around her began to fall inward on themselves.

"Merena! Let's get out of here!" Adrie's voice echoed.

No! Don't move, you're safe... Merena covered her head and stayed as still as she possibly could, waiting for a rock to crush her and her dreams along with it.

Merena called out, "Don't move, Adrie!" Within seconds, the rocks settled. Glancing up, Merena was amazed to see that not a single rock lay in front of her. In fact, it looked as if they had made a path for her. *Follow the path...* Standing up, Merena forgot about Adrie. All she cared about was the voice inside her head. *Go on... Take the sphere deeper...* The further Merena went the less aware she became. She could feel the ice ball piercing her hand. It was almost as if it was connected to her. Like she was meant to find it. Nearing the place where the cave ended, Merena was surprised to see a set of stairs that circled down and around the corner. *Keep going...* Trusting the voice, Merena took a step down the stairs. She felt absolutely no emotion, as if she was merely following orders.

The stairs seemed to continue on forever like a line without a point. Nearly five minutes later, Merena was met with stone-like ground. Turning the corner, Merena was met with water. A large round pool of glistening water. Certain the water was calling her, Merena let her body take control. Merena took two steps that sent her flying through the air. Water crashed into her body, feeling her up like a well does an empty jug. The icy sphere pulled her deeper into the water. Merena did not resist, for she felt like her two legs were slowing her down. She waited as the sphere dropped towards a hole in the sand-like floor. *Place it there, Merena... Come on...* Merena's mind begged her to turn around, to stop listening to the voice. Yet her body obeyed it without a second thought. Her arm stung as she pressed the sphere into the hole. The water became restless, swirling around Merena like a whirlpool. For the first time in her life, Merena felt scared of the water, unsure whether it was for her or against her. Struggling to push her way back to the surface, Merena felt a pressure against her lungs. Pain replaced her fear as her lungs threatened to explode. Darkness crept in as Merena got sight of a hand reaching towards her. Her mind spun and seemed to slip away as she reluctantly grabbed the hand just as her body gave out.

CHAPTER SEVENTEEN

Alone No More

It seemed as if hours had passed as Evalyn awakened from an unwanted sleep. Glancing around, Evalyn felt different, refreshed, more alive than she had ever felt. Her skin was silky smooth, her eyes seemed as if they could see miles further, and her body begged to continue on her journey. All around Evalyn was destruction, the cave that had tumbled down on her seemed to have been crushed. *Why hadn't she been crushed with it?* The coral was no longer in its perfect locations, but uprooted and dimmed. A sudden thought rushed through Evalyn's mind. *Wasn't there someone else in the cave? Did they survive this disaster?*

Unsure of where to look, Evalyn headed to the last standing object within a mile. It was a giant pointed rock that peeked out from the surface. Rubbing her hands against the ancient stone, Evalyn wondered about its age. It probably had so many unspoken stories to tell. Evalyn gave thanks for the rock, for it allowed her a steadier look at her surroundings. To the west, Evalyn saw no one. To the south, nothing but a possible pod of dolphins. To the East lay emptiness. Slowly, Evalyn turned to the north. Nothing. Evalyn's heart sank along with her body against the side of the rock. Maybe she had imagined the mergirl's voice.

A sudden cough took Evalyn by surprise. Glancing down, Evalyn nearly screamed with joy. Lying below her was a gorgeous mermaid. Quickly swimming to her side, Evalyn rested beside her.

"I knew I had seen someone!" Evalyn exclaimed. A confused look crossed the dazed mergirl's face as she sat up.

"You're ok! I'm ok!" The mergirl burst from the rock and spun in a great circle, "I feel amazing!" Adelia joined the mergirl in the celebration.

"Why'd you say that I was ok?" Evalyn questioned.

The mergirl grabbed Evalyn's shoulders, "Last time I saw you, you were a sight. Rock dust covered your face and there were scratches and scars all over your body! But now, you look perfectly new!"

"Really!" Evalyn exclaimed, "My name is Evalyn by the way."

Adelia reached out her hand in greeting as she replied with, "Mine's Adelia."

The mergirls continued to spin with excitement as they exchanged their stories of who they were.

Unaware, the mergirls continued to talk as the sea began to rebuild itself from their energy. Power surges escaped from their hair hitting corals and returning them to their rightful place. The ocean fed off the girls as it joined in on their excitement, creating a whirlpool around them.

As the girls slowed, so did the ocean, for there was a rare harmony present in the northern hemisphere, a sudden peace that hadn't been there for over a decade. Little did the mergirls know, the power surges they were giving off were being sensed by every creature in the Northern Sea Kingdom: the weakened eels, the starving squids, the fearful mergirls, and the terrifying ruler, the King of the Northern Sea Kingdom.

The King sat high on his throne scanning the waves. His muscles pulsing with fury causing his tattooed skin to pulse. Usually on days like this he would marvel at his masterpiece. He lived in a kingdom that served him and only him. He was the only thriving creature in this part of the ocean. In fact, he liked to think that he was the only thriving creature in the entirety of the great blue sea. However, today the seas were unsteady, restless, and longing for something. *But what? Why did he feel so icky inside?* Something or someone was coming, and he promised himself that he would be ready. For this was his throne, his kingdom, and he would not let anyone take it away. He had risked and done too much just to have it all slip through his fingers again.

"Come, whoever you are... I'll be ready," the King whispered.

Diamonds, Jewels, and More

Merena tasted her dry tongue as she came to. Her body ached and felt damp. Opening her eyes, Merena was welcomed by a concerned looking Adrie.

"Ah! Merena, you've come to! I was afraid I was going to have to leave you here with the treasure!" Adrie sat Merena up on what she believed was a rock. *Or maybe her back was leaning against a wall?* Reality sucked in like a gust of wind.

"Wait! You were gonna leave me?" Merena exclaimed as she looked into Adrie's eyes.

With a wave of her hand, Adrie turned around, "Look!"

Merena noticed a bright glow on Adrie's face as she stood up. Merena let out a gasp. Before her were three giant piles of gold, silver, diamonds, and jewels.

"Where did this come from?" Merena asked.

Adrie had begun stuffing her clothes with the fine treasure, "The wall broke the moment I pulled you out of the water! It was crazy! Rocks flying everywhere! It was like bang! Smash! Kaboom! I thought we were goners!"

Merena glanced around at the rocks that had fallen from the previous wall of the cave. They had crashed into the water pool and piled up on each other all over the cave. Everywhere lay rock debris, except for where Adrie and Merena sat. *Merena...* It was the voice again. Merena rushed past the treasure-consumed Adrie and over the pile of treasure, placing the palms of her hands on the rock wall behind the glistening treasure. *Keep coming Merena...*

Slowing, Merena applied pressure to the wall. The cool wall seemed to want to resist Merena's touch. Closing her eyes, Merena focused. *Why couldn't she say no to the voice? Where was this voice coming from? If it wasn't the pool or the treasure, then what was it?*

Merena, hurry! Without thinking, Merena pushed with all her might. Just as she thought she was going to have to try a different way; the wall gave in. The momentum sent Merena flying headfirst into darkness. Afraid she was about to tumble one hundred feet downward, Merena tried to tuck into a ball. But it was in vain. Within two seconds, Merena hit a stone floor with a thud.

"Um, Merena," Adrie called out, "Why'd you do that?"

Merena glanced around in confusion. *Why was she pushing on the wall?* She couldn't remember. Merena reached out her hand to stand. The mark of Queen Ramona was glowing unusually bright. *Had it been glowing this whole time?* A cold object came in contact with Merena's hand.

"I think I found something," Merena exclaimed. The jingle of Adrie's treasure-filled clothing rang from above. Merena's eyes were blinded by a light as Adrie flung her legs over the side of the hole Merena had created. As her eyes focused, Merena realized she had fallen ten feet. Merena waited for Adrie to do something but she just sat there in a daze.

"Adrie?" Merena asked as she stood up and knocked the dust off herself.

"Merena, we're rich!" Adrie exclaimed, "Look!!"

Merena turned around. Her body froze as she caught a glimpse of the sight in front of her. High piles of golden treasure met her eyes. It seemed to go on for miles. Adrie jumped down into the pit, nearly landing on Merena.

Adrie jogged into the treasure-infested room, "Come on! Let's take some for ourselves, before Queen Ramona..." A ringing stung in Merena's ears and a pain swept through her arms at the mention of Ramona's name. Grabbing her arm, Merena slumped to the ground. *Merena... Remember anything that is yours is mine... Bring that treasure back full without a single missing piece or else...*

Merena's pain immediately subsided as she stared ahead. *Had Queen Ramona been the voice? Surely not. If so, was she the voice the entire time?* Adrie was already filling her boots because her hats, jackets, and shirt seemed to be full. Merena silently admired how detailed Adrie stuffed her clothing, so a normal person would not realize that she was caring treasure. Merena sighed. Adrie was going to be so disappointed when she told her they would have to return all of this to Queen Ramona.

Merena lifted herself up and slowly made her way to the treasure obsessed Adrie. Merena walked over the treasure, trying her best not to disturb any of it. Awkwardly standing before Adrie, who was currently climbing a pile of treasure, Merena felt sick. *Why was she doing what the voice was telling her? Was it due to fear? Authority? A self-want?*

"Um, Adrie..." Merena called out.

Without a glance downward, Adrie slid down the pile, causing gold coins and jewels to tumble at Merena's feet.

"Can you believe this?" Adrie exclaimed as she held up a tiara that glistened as if it had a million diamonds upon its surface.

"I ... Adrie ... listen..." Merena began.

Adrie threw a handful of gold in the air and spun around, "Why the long face, Merena? We get to take part of this gold for ourselves, then some for the crew, and then some more for us!" Adrie jumped back into a pile of gold and started making snow-gold angels.

"Listen, we have to give all of this to Queen Ramona," Merena felt her eyes shifting.

Adrie froze, seemingly freezing time with her. Slowly, Adrie's face began to fill with crimson. She rose slightly, knocking away a large purple jewel.

"This is ours, it's mine... I technically saw it first..." Adrie was now face to face with Merena, glaring into her soul.

"Why are you doing this, Merena?" Adrie clenched her fist together.

Merena felt unable to control herself as if her body was not her own.

"She'll know... She knows," Merena replied, "She always does when I'm around." Merena flinched as she realized the marking on her hand was glowing with great intensity.

Adrie sighed, "Fine, we'll give Queen Ramona some of the treasure... Her share of the treasure."

Good... Now hurry, Bring it all and fast. I must speak with you, the voice echoed in Merena's head once again. As she watched Adrie begin to stuff her bags with jewels, Merena fell to the ground, weak. *How much longer could she live under the power of Queen Ramona?*

CHAPTER NINETEEN

An Uncertain Future

A magical energy surged through Adelia unlike any other. She felt as if she was feeding off of Evalyn's energy. She had never met someone so creative and funny as Evalyn.

"...and that's how I got here. Sure, I am going to miss my dolphin family, but I know I'll find my original family one day. I mean, I'm closer than I've ever been," Evalyn sighed as she laid back on the rock and stared toward the surface of the ocean.

Joining Evalyn, Adelia smiled, "It's so cool that you grew up with dolphins. I've never even talked to a dolphin, but you learned how to play an instrument from one! That's so cool!"

"I guess. I've never gotten to play in front of a real crowd though. All because of the fears of my adopted family. But it's my dream, you know, to play in front of thousands of mermaids. I wanna inspire them with my songs…" Evalyn sat up, "What's your dream?"

"Other than to find my family?" Adelia thought for a second. No one had ever asked her what her dreams were before, "I guess I want to travel. I wanna see all the places in the books that I've read about. No more imagining, I wanna do the things that the heroines in my books have done. I wanna see the human world and play fetch with a polar bear."

Evalyn giggled, "Play fetch with a polar bear? How would you do that?"

"I don't know, but I can't wait to try!" Adelia laughed at the thought of having legs and a pet with four of them. That would be bizarre.

"So, where are you heading?" Evalyn asked.

"The Northern King…"

Evalyn cut Adelia off, "No way! I'm heading there too! You know it's really dangerous there now."

"I know the kingdoms are tense between each other right now," Adelia replied.

"They are declaring war. That's why I had to leave," Evalyn sighed as she glanced toward her previous home.

Fear snuck into Adelia's mind. *War? What had she gotten herself into?*

"I've got to find my family, but I don't know where to start," her voice shook with emotion.

"We can do it together; we both blend in pretty well with the environment. We can use that to our advantage, but we probably need to get going," Evalyn touched Adelia 's hand sending an electric shock through their bodies. Neither of them thought much about it; maybe they had imagined it.

"Let's go," Evalyn said as Adelia began swimming lower towards the sand.

Swimming on her back, Adelia studied Evalyn. Something about her seemed so familiar. Maybe it was because she was the first mermaid she had ever met from the Northern Sea

Kingdom or maybe it was something else. Adelia just couldn't put her finger on it, "So, tell me more about your family. Maybe I can help you and you can help me."

"I don't know much. Actually, I don't know anything," Evalyn's eyes studied the distance as if she was trying to remember something, anything, "I was left alone at the bottom of the sea, where Tank, one of the dolphins, found me. All I had with me was this shell woven in my hair."

Adelia's heart quickened as she quickly unwove the shell she had been left with when she was a merbaby. Gripping her shell in her hand, Adelia's heart nearly stopped as Evalyn revealed a nearly identical shell.

"Is everything alright?" Evalyn questioned. Adelia looked at the shell in her own hand and realized her body had stopped moving.

She looked into the wondering eyes of Evalyn and whispered, "I was left alone at the bottom of the sea. All I had was *this* shell woven in my hair." Adelia watched as excitement appeared on Evalyn's face.

"How old are you? When were you found?" Evalyn questioned as she held her shell up to Adelia's.

"I'm ten years old," Adelia floated to the seafloor causing the sand to unsettle around her, "I was found ten years ago."

Evalyn pulled Adelia back up, "I thought you looked familiar! You're me. I mean I'm you! We're…"

"Twins…" Adelia whispered as realization kicked in, "We're sisters! You're my family!" As Evalyn pulled Adelia in for a giant hug an energy surge burst from within them, so strong that it launched them a hundred yards apart from each other. Their energy sent yet another wave two hundred miles per hour in every direction. However, this wave did not cause destruction. This wave, for a split second, made everything back to the way it used to be. For a split second, the Northern Sea Kingdom was full of elegant, tall buildings. Mermaids sang in the street, and balance was restored to the ocean. Above the waters, the clouds let the sunshine through, adding warmth to the cold hearts of the humans. But just like a forgotten memory, it was all gone in seconds. The broken world returned.

❧

It had become a cloudy night as Merena threw her legs over the side of *The Siphon*. Merena's body ached with exhaustion. Never had she walked that far and long with such a heavy thing upon her back. Adrie and Merena had taken as much treasure as they could possibly carry with them as they journeyed back to the vessel. However, just as Merena had expected, Queen Ramona had sent her minions to gather up the rest. Anger was all Merena was receiving from Adrie at the moment. She wished she could go back and not listen to the tiny voice in her head, but it somehow seemed to control her every action.

Nearly crawling to her quarters, Merena ignored the yells and cheers of the pirates around her. She didn't care about the treasure nor did she want to capture her kind. All Merena wanted was to return to the sea and find the truth. She prayed that one day she'd find out who was behind the scars on her skin. *Why had they taken her parents away from her? Had they destroyed her kingdom just like…*

A sudden wave hit *The Siphon* with such impact that it tossed Merena onto her back, causing her to gaze up at the sky. For a split second, Merena thought she saw stars. Not one or two like normal, but millions of stars. Bright, brilliant stars that shone with such pride. But as the boat stopped rocking, the clouds came back to cover the brilliant night sky. Lying there, Merena didn't want to move; she wanted the stars to come back.

A sharp familiar pain stung Merena's leg. Glancing down, she watched as her leg glowed through her pants. Merena said a silent "sorry" to whoever else bore the same scar as she now had upon her leg.

Clip Clop Clip Clop. Merena hung her head at the sound of the footsteps of her mistress. *Couldn't this have waited until morning?*

❧

The King of the Northern Sea Kingdom pulled his trident out of the tail of his fourth servant this month. Anger pulsed through his skin as he watched his servant's body be consumed into the trident. For a moment he had thought he had lost everything. The kingdom, for a second, was peaceful, musical. It made him want to throw up. *What kind of monster was trying to fool with his mind?* He did not appreciate it one bit.

"Your Highness, Sir," a small blobfish carrying a letter entered into the King's courtroom.

"Yes?" the King raised his eyebrow at the ugly creature. It made him happy such things resided in his land.

"A message," the blobfish shakingly handed the King the rolled-up letter, "from the Southern and Western Sea Kingdoms."

The King nearly laughed at the perfectly tied red bow that sealed the letter. Such perfectionism. Power surged through the King's bones as he unrolled the letter. His eyes skimmed it with satisfaction.

"King… We have decided… War … in two weeks … be prepared to be overtaken … blah … blah … blah," the King pillowed over in laughter, "Overtake me? The most powerful king to rule the Northern Seas. Don't they know I possess the most powerful trident in the land. The Eastern Sea Kingdom has Nature, the Southern Sea Kingdom has Happiness, and the Western Sea Kingdom has Passion. I control the balance between all of these, between all of the seas, between the creatures, and even between the humans. I am the keeper of balance and these kingdoms haven't even seen what it is like to be without me. Nothing can be accomplished without me. I'd like to see them try to come against me."

Evalyn shook off the sand that had landed on her tail. *What was that?* Glancing around, Evalyn searched for her newly found sister. They had only realized they were twins for how long? And they'd already lost each other.

"Adelia," Evalyn's voice echoed through the water as Adelia came into sight about seventy yards south of where they had previously been swimming.

"I'm coming!" Adelia hollered, but quickly realized she probably shouldn't have yelled when they were trying to go unnoticed.

"What happened?" Adelia asked as they caught up with each other.

"I have no clue. I was hoping you'd know. You are the smart one," Evalyn said as she gasped for air, "That sure knocked the wind out of me."

"Yeah, we better get going. We don't wanna stay in one place for too long," Adelia exclaimed.

Evalyn nodded as she followed Adelia north. Neither girl was sure what they were going to find nor what to expect in the kingdom where they were from. Each kept high hopes, but a fear of being disappointed hid in the back of each of the young girls' minds.

Merena stood up slowly as the footsteps stopped behind her. She wasn't sure what Queen Ramona was going to say or do to her. Turning around, Merena was met with a soggy looking Queen Ramona. *Had she fallen off the boat again?*

"Look at me!" Queen Ramona cried, "I'm soaked to the bone!" Personally, Merena wanted to laugh, but she held the temptation in.

"Listen here, Merena," Queen Ramona stomped her foot in frustration, "I want to know if you delivered all the treasure to me that you found." Heart quickening, Merena felt a sudden illness fall upon her. She glanced toward a glaring Adrie. Merena knew that Adrie had taken quite a bit of treasure for herself, more than she had even told Merena.

"Um…" Merena fought to form words but she couldn't. *How could she possibly turn in her only friend?*

A friend? Is Adrie really your friend? The voice returned. *She would betray you in an instant. She's only here for the treasure.* Merena watched as Ramona's staff glowed in connection with the voice in her head and the mark upon her skin. Queen Ramona gripped her staff hard with a terrifying grin upon her face.

"I can read your mind yah know," Queen Ramona turned around, "You!" She pointed straight at Adrie, "You have betrayed us all. You selfish little brat!"

"No!" Merena screamed as she crumpled to the deck in pain.

"Silence!" Ramona slammed her staff down upon the ground. Merena felt as if her voice had been ripped from within her. She couldn't make a sound; she couldn't even move her lips. Merena watched helplessly as Adrie backed up in fear.

"You have Merena to thank for turning you in, Adrie," Queen Ramona laughed as she pinned Adrie against the boat wall, "all she had to do was think about turning you in and I had access to her thoughts. I don't make her think or do anything evil. I only encourage her original intentions." Queen Ramona held Adrie's chin with her icy fingers. Purple smoke released from Queen Ramona's face and into Adrie's. It seemed to suck the life out of the poor girl. Merena watched as Adrie's eyes turned to dull ice. Queen Ramona turned Adrie to face her pirate crew. Adrie struggled to escape, but she was too weak.

Adrie's skin was beginning to turn a pale blue as Queen Ramona laughed, "This is a prime example of the consequences of being a trader. Just because she found the treasure first, she assumed it belonged to her."

"All of you!" Queen Ramona commanded, "Remember this day. For on this day you were shown what happens to someone who doesn't respect their queen. And you, Merena, remember this day as the day that you finally realized that you were merely a servant to me. You are worthless and no longer needed. Just like Adrie."

Queen Ramona pulled the limp Adrie towards the plank of the ship. Screams of regret and fear exploded from within Merena, but there was nothing she could do. This was all her fault.

Everyone on the ship watched, stunned, as Queen Ramona dragged the helpless Adrie to the edge of the plank.

"Would anyone like to do the honors...? Who am I kidding?" Queen Ramona joked as she shoved Adrie off the side of *The Siphon* and into the deep blue sea.

CHAPTER TWENTY

Prisoner

An eerie feeling swept through the twin mergirls as they ventured closer to the Northern Sea Kingdom. Skeleton bones, rotting seaweed, and sickening fish were the only things in sight for what seemed like miles. About two miles back was the last coral reef the mergirls had seen. It seemed that there was nothing alive here. Neither girl dared to say a word for they feared an eel or killer shark would overhear and come searching for lunch.

Adelia's heart quickened as a crumbling stone gate came into sight. There was no sign, no gatekeeper, no nothing near the gate.

"Is this it?" Evalyn whispered.

"Yeah, it resembles the pictures from a book I read on the Northern Sea Kingdom," Adelia said barely over a whisper.

"Well, what are we waiting for? Let's go find our parents," Evalyn tried to seem excited, but she was nearly shaking with fright.

"We're just gonna waltz right in?" Adelia questioned, "Won't we be killed or something?" Adelia looked around. *What else were they supposed to do?*

Evalyn pointed towards a small opening on the side of a medium-sized mountain, "let's stay in there tonight. It's late and I'm kinda tired."

"Ok," Adelia replied.

Heart racing, Adelia let Evalyn venture into the dark hole first. She prayed that no one else wanted to stay there tonight as well. The cave was dark and Adelia feared they would run into someone or something.

Reaching to grab Evalyn's hand, Adelia nearly jumped out of her tail.

"Your tail's glowing!" Evalyn exclaimed. Glancing down, she watched as her tail too emitted a sapphire blue light that allowed the girls to see where they were going.

"This is so cool! I didn't know I did that! Did you?" Adelia said as she wiggled her tail in front of her face.

"Um, no. This hasn't ever happened to me before. In fact, a lot of things have never happened to me until I met you," Evalyn laughed. The hole they had ventured into opened up into a large dome-shaped room. It was empty of any life form at the moment. In the center of the room lay four unmade shell beds with sheets and pillows thrown randomly. There was a large ice cooler and a shell table with carved coral seats. A homemade chest for clothes and accessories sat against the far wall. Other than that, it was empty.

"This must be someone's home," Adelia expressed as she touched the silky, yet wrinkled sheets on the beds, "I've never slept on a bed with sheets before."

"Look! On Ice Seaweed," Evalyn exclaimed as she opened the large cooler, "I am literally starving!"

"Wait, Evalyn! This isn't ours. We can't take it," Adelia cautioned.

Evalyn sighed, "Not even a bite? Pretty please?"

"No, we will go out in the morning and find food," Adelia said.

"What if they come home?" Evalyn questioned. The question made Adelia think. *Was this merfamily even intending to come back?*

Opening a chest, Adelia's conclusion was confirmed, "How old does that seaweed look?"

"Um, a couple of months, but it's on ice. So it will still be good. Why?" Evalyn replied.

"I don't think this family is ever coming back," Adelia exclaimed.

Swimming towards Adelia, Evalyn questioned, "Why do you say that?"

"Well look, their beds aren't made, their clothes and accessories are gone, and they've got no fresh food. Something must have happened for them to have not returned to such a lovely home.

"Oh my goodness you're right! Look, their lights are burnt out too!" Evalyn exclaimed as she tried turning on the light switch.

Adelia bounced on the bed, "Well we've got a temporary home now. How about some On Ice Seaweed?"

"Are you serious? We can eat it?" Evalyn exclaimed.

"Of course, I'm starving and we don't want it to go to waste, do we?"

Adelia rushed over to the ice cooler, pulled out the frozen seaweed and took a big bite out of one. The crispness of the seaweed tasted like honey candy.

"Here ya go," Adelia tossed Evalyn one as she flopped onto the bed next to her, "I'm so glad we found each other."

"Me too, Adelia. Me too," Evalyn said as she bit into the seaweed snack.

Merena felt as if every part of her body had shattered like a fallen vase. Her mind was blank. Unaware of anything around her, she prayed she could rewind the moments that had just happened. *Was Adrie really gone?* She had only just gotten to know her. Finding all the strength left in her, Merena began crawling to the edge of the boat. Every inch felt like a mile. Maybe Adrie had survived. Maybe she was calling out for help and the waves were draining her. Pulling herself up, Merena heard only the waves of laughter from Queen Ramona and the pirate crew. Wind gushed against Merena's back, threatening to push her overboard.

Merena's eyes scanned the crashing waves, "Adrie!! Adrie!!" No one replied. Stumbling back on the deck in defeat, Merena began to cry. Sea glass rushed from her eyes like a waterfall. It splattered against the deck, gathering the attention of the prideful Queen Ramona.

"Aw, poor Merena," Queen Ramona lifted Merena's head, "I forgot that she was your friend. I'm sorry."

Queen Ramona laughed, "James and Jaxson... Send this pitiful thing down to the dungeon. She is of no use to me anymore. Thank you, Merena, for all your help when it came to finding more mermaids and treasure. But I think we get the gist, just paddle around the deep blue sea until you find a curious mermaid and capture her. So, in reality, I really didn't need you and you've wasted my time. Am I mad I have yet to capture another mermaid like you? Of course. But am I proud that I still have a used-to-be future Queen in my captivity? Of course."

James and Jaxon lifted Merena up and began dragging her towards the all too familiar trap door. Merena felt nauseous as her mind raced back to the day Queen Ramona had first captured her. James pulled open the trap door and Merena looked down into the dark hole of nothingness.

"Oh, Merena," Queen Ramona pulled Merena's face towards her. Queen Ramona's evil eyes felt as if they were piercing a scar upon Merena's skin. Merena fought to look away, but it was as if she was glued to Queen Ramona.

Queen Ramona sighed, "If only you could have been of more use to me, maybe you'd have gotten to see your ... kids, again. But no, Merena. You let me down. So, congratulations, you're no longer my servant. I no longer get to be nice to you. I can do whatever I want to you. Because Merena, you are now my prisoner."

CHAPTER TWENTY-ONE

Scars of the Past, Present, and Future

Merena sat shaking in the cold cell of the ship. James and Jaxson had led her past the captured mermaids and into a damp, dark cell at the far end of *The Siphon*. Every bone in her body screamed of exhaustion. All she wanted to do was lay down and wake up from this terrible nightmare, or at least dream of a better one. Jaxson sat in a rickety old chair outside Merena's cell, while James sat on the floor chewing on a gold coin.

"So, is this even legal?" James spoke up.

Jaxson gave James a questioning look, "What do you mean, is this even legal?"

"Well, yah know, make someone a prisoner without a trial. Like what did she even do? And what's gonna happen to the beauty?" James coughed as he nearly choked on his gold coin.

"I guess you're right. Most people do get a trial, but the queen can do whatever she pleases, I guess," Jaxson replied. Merena wondered if they had forgotten she was still there or if she had ears.

"I mean, a beautiful woman…"

"Mermaid," corrected Jaxson.

"Beautiful mermaid," James continued as he stood up, "shouldn't be behind bars. She should be free. Maybe not all of them, but Merena has served her time. Don't you think?"

Laughter erupted from Jaxson as he joined James by the bars of Merena's cell. Merena felt awkward. She wondered what she looked like to them. *Weak? Smelly? Gross? Probably all three.*

"You're not in love with a fish are yah, James? I mean look at her. Sure she was … ok is, the prettiest mermaid we have ever caught, but Queen Ramona loathes her kind because of the incident," Curiosity struck Merena. *What was he talking about?*

Jaxson laughed, "This is the mermaid that's somehow stopping us from having sunshine all the time. Ah, do you remember those days, James?"

"Jaxson, first off I'm not in love. I just want to make sure everyone gets treated fairly most of the time. And secondly, I suppose you're right, but how does locking her up get us back the sunshine?" James ran his finger across the bars, creating an irritating noise.

"Why don't yah ask the poor thing if ya really wanna know," Jaxson flopped back down into his chair, "I'm taking a nap, so don't be too loud."

Merena buried her head in her arms as she felt James's stare fall upon her. She had no intention of speaking to James.

"So, what are you and your kind going to do to us now," James inquired.

Merena shook her head. She felt as empty as she had ever been. The bit of assurance the ocean had given her earlier that morning seemed to have disappeared.

"So, you're saying nothing will change?" James banged on the cage, causing Merena to glance up.

"Don't you understand the sea is aching to be balanced again? The Northern Sea Kingdom used to be the Kingdom of Balance. We were nearly forgotten about, yet we were the glue! Everything was fine until the morning when *we* met!" Merena's tears rushed from within her.

James laughed, "So, it is our fault. Because we took you and now you're gone. And the sea is unbalanced.

Merena shook her head, "You are not capable of such destruction. You are weak and ignorant at times. I mean, for goodness sake, you fall to your knees to gain the smallest respect from your "Queen," Queen Ramona."

"Excuse me," Jaxson lifted his head from his chest where he had seemingly been sleeping, "She's your queen too and if we didn't destroy the balance, who did?"

"I did," Merena whispered, "My parents were killed, and I wasn't there to protect them. I wasn't where I should have been to protect my kingdom. I stepped out of my place and now my whole kingdom could be in ruins. My fellow mer-folk could be dead, and I did nothing to stop it. All because I ventured above the water for some fresh air."

"And what if you escaped? What would you do to stop the evil force destroying your kingdom?" James questioned.

"Honestly," Merena stared into the eyes of James, "Honestly, I don't know if I even deserve to rule anymore. So much of myself has evaporated into thin air. My parents are gone. I haven't seen my husband in over ten years. And my daughters are missing. My heart is empty and each time I am in the presence of Queen Ramona a part of me slips away," Merena sighed, "I am merely an organism going through the motions in order to stay alive."

Evalyn sat at the edge of her temporary bed. She couldn't sleep. The water was cold and still. Her body felt empty and a longing tugged at her heart. She wanted to continue on her journey. She wanted to enter the Northern Sea Kingdom and find her parents. Shifting her eyes toward her newly-found family, Evalyn let her mind wander. Adelia's chest slowly raised and fell to the heartbeat of the sea. Magic seemed to fill the space between. *How unusual was it that they both were searching for lost parents? Was it true what Lulu said, trust no one? Could she really trust this girl? Was she really her twin sister?* The ocean seemed to say she was.

Stretching her tail, Evalyn swam out of the cave entrance. Breathing in deep, the water refreshed her soul as it released slowly. The ocean seemed to go on for miles without a living organism in sight. Darkness was the only thing that surged with power in this part of the sea. Evalyn feared that the longing within her would result in her becoming a part of the darkness.

"What do you see?" Adelia broke the silence that had begun to creep into Evalyn's soul.

"Nothing," Evalyn replied, "Absolutely nothing."

"I see open water full of answers and explanations. Somewhere out there both us will find the answers we've been looking for," Adelia swam out a little further, "I could find mine tomorrow, while you could find the answers to your dreams in five years. Neither of us knows, but for now, we have each other."

Peace flowed through Evalyn; she was right. Her idea of the future had already changed. She wasn't spending her days reading books about adventures anymore. No, she was writing her own adventure, her own book that maybe someone, just like her, would read.

"Do you wanna leave now?" Adelia questioned.

Looking out at the dark waters, Evalyn sighed. *What was the difference between heading into the Northern Sea Kingdom now or later?* Yes, it would be a bit brighter later, but it was the Northern Sea Kingdom. Its purpose is to stay hidden, not brighten up your day. Maybe some shell lights would be emitting some light once they entered the city, but for now, there was only darkness.

Nodding her head, Evalyn swam forward, "Yes, let's go."

"Good, because I already packed our bags," Adelia replied, holding up two dark blue medium-sized bags.

"Where'd you get those?" Evalyn grabbed one and released the strings that held the opening together.

Flinging her bag against her back, Adelia replied, "Under the beds. I just packed us some snacks and maybe we can collect some rare shells on our way through the Northern Sea Kingdom."

"Nice thinking," Evalyn expressed as she, too, flung her bag onto her back. Taking a deep breath, she wondered if the next day would bring any answers to her decade-old questions.

It felt as if they had been swimming for a hundred miles of devastation. Houses crumbled, parks ruined, and schoolhouses were simply no more. Adelia had dreamed of what the Northern Sea Kingdom would look like. She thought it would be large, elegant, a perfect getaway for someone searching for peace. Yet, the deeper the mergirls swam, the more fear and hopelessness seemed to knock at their heart. As the mergirls entered the main parts of the city, more living beings came into view. Adelia flinched at the sight of the begging merfolk.

Their bones nearly stuck out of their skin, it looked as if they hadn't had a good meal in weeks.

A sudden guilt filled Adelia. She had food on her back. Yet, as the long streets of the Northern Sea Kingdom continued to creep along, she realized there were thousands of needy merfolk on every corner. The merfolk said nothing, but they glared at the mergirls with their eyes. *What were they thinking?* Adelia wasn't sure if she really wanted to know.

"What do we do now?" Evalyn whispered.

Spotting a Crab Cafe, Adelia nodded and mouthed, *This way. Follow my lead.*

Gathering her strength, Adelia swam towards the broken door of the Crab Cafe. Glancing in the window she saw about fifteen crabs, all playing a competitive game of pool.

Just as Adelia was about to press against the door of the cafe, a gush of water swirled her and Evalyn, sending them crashing into the side of a nearly disintegrated building. Adelia struggled as the water pulled them deeper into the seemingly century-old building. Letting the water take control of her body, Adelia felt herself being swept down what felt like a tub-shaped hole in the ground. The water stung her skin as it rushed past her. Her blood felt icy cold and she began to ache.

Just when she felt as if she was going to lose consciousness, the water suddenly stopped. Adelia's body froze. Every part of her seemed to be floating in space, almost as if time itself had stopped. She could not move, nor speak. She could only stare into the darkness. *Or were her eyes closed?*

All of a sudden, a voice as loud as a trumpet filled Adelia's ears, "Good night my sweet, Evalyn and Adelia. When you arise, your time will come." Adelia was suddenly overcome with drowsiness. She struggled to stay awake, to see who owned the soothing voice. Yet it was all in vain, for within seconds darkness filled her mind and she fell into a deep sleep.

The King of the Northern Sea Kingdom held his trident up for examination. He ran his fingers across the detailed designs, not wondering nor caring what they meant or if they did anything. He merely liked the way it complimented his current position. He praised the way it gave him power. And he loved the way it made him feel.

Raising his eyebrows at a sickly, handsome-looking eel, the King got in what he called his power stance. He believed it struck fear in the eyes of anyone beneath him.

"You may speak," the King commanded.

Shaking and spitting electricity, the eel replied, "I wanted to inform you that two strangers entered the borders of the kingdom about three hours ago."

The King laughed, "What are you waiting for? Bring them to me right away. You know the rules. Any unannounced suspicious creatures in the Northern Sea Kingdom must be executed."

The eel sighed, "It was merely two curious mergirls."

The King felt a bang of fear sweep through him. *Were the offspring of his only rival here to avenge his throne?* The daughters of the only merman who had one-upped him in everything he had done in life.

"Is there an older mermaid, about my age, with them as well?" the King held his breath in anticipation.

"No, just two Northern Mergirls," the eel answered.

So, she is still missing, the King thought.

"Bring these mergirls to me at once, for they are a danger to us all!" The King commanded. The eel lowered his hand, in an attempt to avoid eye contact with the King.

He frowned at the fearful looking eel, "What is it?"

"They are gone," the eel managed to say.

Anger bubbled up inside the King's chest, "Gone!! Explain yourself!" The King pointed the trident at the heart of the poor eel.

"They... Um..." the eel's eyes drifted every which way, "They were going to the Crab Cafe when a gust of water sent them flying into one of the abandoned buildings. Once the sand had settled, we searched the damaged building, but they had gone. Vanished into thin air. I am sorry, your majesty."

"I am sorry, too. Because you know what you have to do. The law clearly states if one disappoints the King, they must be executed," the King didn't think twice as he pressed the trident into the chest of the terrified eel.

❧

Merena had begun to think that Queen Ramona really had nothing to do with her, other than sending her minions down to beg her to stop the cloudy weather and rough seas. Not a day passed that James or Jaxson would not come down to her cell. However, it had been ten marks upon the wall since Queen Ramona had come to see her and twenty-one marks since she had been destined to live her days upon the wet, wooden floor of the cell. Every hour it seemed that another mermaid was flung into the main cellar room without a tail and a hopeless face. Nearly three times a day a new scar appeared upon Merena's body. She shuddered as the familiar pain of a new scar stung in her chest. She grabbed her heart and shed a tear for whoever had lost their lives because of her. Feeling the scars upon her face, Merena feared the thought of seeing them, for she knew she must look horrific.

Listening to the muffled sounds of male pirate voices and the constant drip of water droplets, Merena wondered if this was the way she would live out the rest of her days. *Was her destiny to waste away in a dungeon at sea? Would she ever get a chance to take her place the history books had prewritten for her? Was there a chance she could live out the days with her dear husband that she had dreamt about?* Laying her head into her lap, Merena began to wail in despair and agony. She let her tears fall until she had nothing left. Until her nearly empty heart ran dry, and her eyes became heavy with exhaustion. Merena grasped the floor as she drifted off to sleep remembering what it had been like to have someone else help carry the weight of her soul.

CHAPTER TWENTY-TWO

An Unexpected Ally

Five Years Later

Evalyn struggled to connect her thoughts as a heaviness began to release her. Her body felt numb and darkness was the only thing she could see. Within seconds, a sting, like a thousand needles poking at her skin, swept across her body. Finally, her eyes opened to a slightly dimmed room. Slowly sitting up, she flinched as she swatted away a cobweb that had been built upon her face. *How long had she been asleep?* As she stretched her seemingly ancient bones, Evalyn realized she was lying in a giant oyster shell. No wonder her back ached. Evalyn tried to make sense of where she was. It seemed to be some sort of cave. Two tiny coral lanterns hung upon the rock walls of the circular-shaped room. The lights emitted just enough light for Evalyn to see that there was at least one exit to the room. It was straight ahead and narrow.

A frown crossed her face as she glanced at her tail. It looked different. Maybe it was because she was lying in a shell, but it almost seemed larger to her. Releasing herself from the shell, Evalyn felt her bones crack and moan as if they were begging her to return to her slumber.

Spinning around, Evalyn realized another shell rested back to back with hers. Just as Evalyn began to swim around to the other side, a dark head full of hair popped into her sight.

"Adelia!" Evalyn exclaimed as she rushed to hug the confused-looking face. As the two girls embraced, a surge of energy passed through them. It seemed to bring peace and comfort back into their hearts and souls.

"Where are we?" Adelia asked as she rubbed her eyes, "I feel like I've been lying in the same position for years."

"Whoa!" Evalyn whispered as she took in the beautiful maiden before her. Adelia wasn't a child anymore. Her tail had developed with mystical details, her hair nearly glowed with strength, and her eyes were larger than ever. Adelia glanced up and nearly backed away when she too saw the transformation of her "new" friend.

"When did you get all grown up?" Adelia questioned. Shocked, she overtook Evalyn. *How long had they really been asleep?*

"You're all grown up too," Evalyn whispered, "I mean the last thing I remember was searching for our parents near … was it a cafe? There was a gust of wind and then darkness."

Adelia nodded, "I remember that too, except I vaguely remember a voice … maybe?"

"Oh, I do too…" Evalyn scrunched her eyebrows in thought, "I don't remember what it said."

"Me neither," Adelia sighed, "So what do we do now?"

Evalyn thought for a moment. They had gotten in here one way, so that meant they could get out, "Well I guess we just continue our search. Maybe this set us back a bit, but at least we are stronger now."

"You're right. So which way should we go? Right or up?" Adelia asked.

Looking over her head, Evalyn saw the second exit. It looked as if it could almost suck one right in, destined to never return.

"Good morning ladies," a harmonic voice broke the girls' trains of thought. Squinting their eyes towards the tunnel nearest to the seafloor, the twins felt their bodies freeze in uncertainty. Reaching for Adelia's hand, Evalyn kept her eyes focused on the tunnel above. Adelia's hands were like ice as they shakily grasped Evalyn's. Evalyn felt a pulsing fear erupt from within her. The dark cave above slowly began to emit a strange light.

Blinking, Evalyn watched as an outline of a mermaid began to form as the voice spoke up, "It is time."

❈

A heavy force seemed to hold Merena's hand down as she fought to add another mark to her prison wall. Every day for five years, Merena had added a tally mark in order to keep herself sane. Somehow, she saw each day as a victory. She had kept Queen Ramona from winning for five thousand eight hundred and forty days of her life. Even if one thousand eight hundred and twenty-five of those days were in the same place, doing the same thing, over and over again. Merena's body had become numb. She no longer became hungry, her tears were dry, and her thoughts were choppy and never seemed to finish. She was merely breathing, hoping for someone to step in and change her fate. She was doing everything in her power to stay alive and wait. Something inside her dared her to keep fighting, to never give in to the thoughts of James, Jaxson, and the ruthless Queen Ramona.

Clung! Merena's eyes shifted upward towards the sound. Her vision had become weak over the past year and every little sound seemed to irritate her. *Another capture,* Merena thought. Within seconds, her expectations were confirmed as the cries of a lost mergirl filled her ears. Oh, how she wished she could comfort her, but she knew it would be in vain. *What would she even say? You are stuck here forever, and Queen Ramona is basically going to suck all the magic and uniqueness out of you until you look like me. Or our only hope lies in the hands of someone else?*

Merena felt her hands begin to shake violently as the all too familiar footsteps neared her prison. Her body ached to get closer to the source that Queen Ramona held. It was like a severe necessity that had been neglected and ignored for too long.

"You're still alive?" Queen Ramona's voice cracked as she stepped from the shadows. Merena did not even attempt to produce a sound. It seemed she had lost it years ago.

Queen Ramona huffed, "Well, I thought you would be pleased to know that we caught our eight hundredth mermaid today! Isn't that just wonderful?" Queen Ramona spun her sceptre with her fingers causing an eerie glow to emit from the sapphire jewel within it. Merena's eyes fixed upon the jewel. The rotating sapphire reminded her of something, yet she couldn't put her finger on it. She admired the unique cracked side that almost seemed as if it fit somewhere else. Merena's body begged to touch it, but Queen Ramona merely stood and stared at the sight of Merena's decaying spirit.

"I've never told you how I gained this mighty power, have I Merena?" Queen Ramona said as she glared at her sceptre. Merena nearly rolled her eyes. She did not care, she only wanted her to go away. She wanted all of this to go away.

Queen Ramona touched the tip of her sceptre, "It was destiny, I tell you. When I was quite young, merely a princess, I was sitting at the edge of my favorite cliff, staring out at the sea. I did this every day for years. I even thought I saw a mermaid once or twice. Well, on this particular day, there was a different feeling in the air. I was scanning the sea when all of a sudden the beautiful blue skies turned black. Thunder erupted as a giant hurricane exploded from the seas. Part of me wonders if I should have run away. I didn't though, and that's when I saw a sapphire stone shoot out of the water. At first, I thought it was nothing but then it started flying towards me. Gusts of wind pounded against my body. Yet, I felt no fear, so I stood and waited. The sapphire slowed as it approached me. I reached out and grabbed it. The wind around me, and only me, froze in place. A great power surged through me. I liked it and I believed it liked me. Maybe it even chose me. I immediately had this sceptre forged to fit the stone perfectly. After that day everything was different. I needed no one."

Queen Ramona scanned Merena up and down, "There's not much left in you, is there Merena?" Queen Ramona laughed, "Soon your entire soul will belong to me and I will possess the power of a merqueen."

Merena's eyes glared at the wicked sight in front of her, yet her body wanted to obey, to bow, to submit before Queen Ramona.

"Don't fight it," Queen Ramona said as she thumped her sceptre upon the wooden floor of *The Siphon*, "Give yourself to me." A violent shaking took over Merena's body as the mark upon her skin glowed. Her mind began to race. Her daughters, her husband, her mother, and her father all flashed before her eyes. A pain struck her heart as Queen Ramona released the sceptre from the ground.

"I'll be back and when I am, I think it will be my very last visit with you, Merena," Queen Ramona smiled and hit her sceptre upon the ground sending Merena's body flopping against the prison wall. Merena collapsed in defeat as a pain rang through her mind. *Where was she? What had she just been thinking?* Merena closed her eyes as she heard the echo of high heel footsteps faded away into the distance.

The King of the Northern Sea Kingdom sat smirking high on his throne. For the past five years, the waters had been absent of any annoyances. There had been no interruption to his successful, well thought out, magnificent plan of ruling the entirety of the four sea kingdoms. The sand beneath his feet had already begun to rot and grow dark with lack of nutrients. It was only time before it would begin to spread out of his kingdom.

The King only laughed when his minions would return saying the other kingdoms were threatening to declare war. First off, they had been saying that for years. Nothing had come out of it. The King assumed it was because of his new army: five hundred thousand bloodthirsty megalodons. Where had he gotten that many sharks? The King promised to never say, for it was his own little secret. His prized possession, other than the trident, of course.

As King, he tried hard not to dwell on the past. Yes, maybe the disappearance of the two mergirls a couple of years ago disturbed him every now and then. But he chose to ignore it. To take his time with his despicable plan and to love every ounce of evil running through his veins.

⁂

Adelia felt the warm grasp of Evalyn's fingers as the strange mermaid came into the light of the cave. The mermaid had dark, thick, jet black hair. The light from the cave seemed to reflect the mermaid's slight blue highlights that made it seem as if she were glowing. *Or was it possible that she really was glowing?* Her tail was a dark coral blue with an excessive number of jewels, pearls, and accessories that detailed her tail in an almost jumbled, but pleasing, chaos. Her eyes seemed to once have shined with curiosity; however, the light blue eyes that stared at the twins now seemed ancient and full of life. The mysterious mermaid swam with grace and demanded power even in a powerless room. She circled Adelia and Evalyn, letting the diamonds upon her neck and the crystals around her wrist glisten with significance.

"Good morning, girls," the mermaid said when she reached full circle around them. Adelia admired the warmth and nurturing voice that escaped the mermaid. It seemed to fill her up inside. No desire to speak seemed to be within Adelia. Any fear Adelia was feeling seconds before had melted away.

She seemed to instantly trust the stranger before her. All she wanted to do was lie down and listen to whatever this mermaid had to say.

"You've been sleeping quite a long time," the mermaid continued, "I'll bet you are quite famished."

Evalyn frowned, "Who are you? Why are we…"

"You must have loads of questions. I mean look at yourself. You don't even recognize your own tail, I assume," the mermaid interrupted, "Please let us make our way to my dining room and get to know each other a little. Then and only then will I explain the great weight that has been thrust upon you two."

Adelia began to swim forward but Evalyn pulled her back, "Why should we trust you?"

"Why, Evalyn, you don't nor should you, have a reason to trust me," the mermaid smiled, "But you both are seeking a truth that I have an answer to. And where else would you go? You are in my home. It would be rude of you to disregard the feast I have prepared for you." A quick thought crossed Adelia's mind. *How did this mermaid know when they would awaken?* A grumbling sound in her stomach interrupted any questions forming in Adelia's mind.

Adelia's cheeks turned pink with embarrassment, "I am starved, Evalyn. Can't we go?"

Evalyn scanned the mermaid in front of her up and down before saying a word, "We don't even know her name and she knows ours. We're kinda at a disadvantage here."

"Like I said, we will talk over dinner," the mermaid waved the girls towards the tunnel where she had emerged, "Please follow me."

Adelia nodded Evalyn onward as the woman disappeared into the tunnel. Evalyn gave a reluctant glare, but slowly nodded her head ok. Adelia swam forward, determined to catch up with the mermaid before she disappeared deeper into the tunnel. Adelia's skin scraped against rocks and shells as she felt her way through the darkening cave. Just as she thought she had lost her a glow began to emit from her hair. Turning, she smiled as Evalyn possessed the same magical glow. *I could get used to this.*

Evalyn's eyes glowed with fascination as she studied her friend before her with great curiosity. *Was the mystery mermaid really going to explain the burning questions within her? Or was she simply going to cover them up with a new bandage of explanations? Was this mermaid even trustworthy?*

Evalyn's mind was on high alert expecting the worst as the two mermaids continued to follow the stranger deeper into the tunnel. The tunnel continued to grow narrower and Evalyn was beginning to scrape herself on the shells that poked out of the cave walls. Squeezing herself around a sharp corner, Evalyn nearly cried out as a shell impaled her side. Holding her side, she half expected to see blood, yet she did not. Glancing down, she watched as a glow shone from beneath her hand. She felt a sting and an overwhelming relaxation as she lifted her hand. There was no wound. There was no scar. *How curious,* Evalyn thought.

The strange mermaid's body, in the eyes of Evalyn, quickly turned into a silhouette as a bright light formed in the distance. Urging Adelia to swim a little faster, Evalyn's heart quickened. *What was destined for them on the other side?*

Adelia's eyes widened as she swam into a magnificent underground room. Near the center of the room, two elegant pillars seemed to hold the ceiling up. A grand dome with exquisite details filled the ceiling. Curtains of gold draped across the glistening sapphire walls. Jewels stuck out from the walls as if they were in a trophy case, waiting to be admired. A table with thirty-four elegant, dark blue, velvet chairs stretched across the narrow room. The table had every place setting imaginable with golden, polished silverware. Candles, coral, and jewels all delicately added to the masterpiece laid before Adelia and Evalyn. Waiters hustled in and out carrying loads of delicious food and placing them upon the table.

Adelia's stomach growled as she saw seaweed noodles with a blue sauce, a vibrantly colored salad with a mix of kelp and sea lettuce, and crunchy, seagrass fries. The strange mermaid motioned the girls to the far end of the table where the majority of the food had been placed. The woman placed herself at the head of the table and nodded for the mergirls to take a seat on either side of her. Adelia allowed Evalyn to sit on the right side, as she slid into the seat on the left. It was extremely comfortable and cozy. She watched as the waiters quickly served her reasonable portions of each variety of food before her. Her previously clear plate turned into one full of greens, reds, and blues. Each one of the mermaids' tall glasses were filled to the top with an orange substance that Adelia had never seen before. The strange mermaid seemed to be waiting for the waiters to leave as they gathered the leftover food that had not touched the plates of the mermaids. Adelia glanced at Evalyn, who looked silently overwhelmed and starved as she stared at the plate before her.

"Now that we are alone, I shall say grace…" the harmonic voice of the mermaid echoed through the room.

CHAPTER TWENTY-THREE

Family History

Evalyn sighed as she leaned back into a large cushioned chair that had been placed in a small sitting area in the far-left corner of the elegant dining room. Evalyn had not noticed it when she had first come in. The dinner had been lovely, even though no one had spoken a word to each other. It had been rather peaceful and extremely satisfying for the starving mergirls. Evalyn felt that all her tension had disappeared with the food that was upon her plate and she was now beginning to trust the mermaid supplying her needs. Adelia and the strange mermaid also sat in identical tall, sapphire-colored, cushioned chairs next to Evalyn. Their vision was directed to a coral reef that danced with life as tiny fish swam in and out through what seemed like an exit to the outside world. Glancing toward the mysterious mermaid, Evalyn was slightly shocked to realize she had been studying her.

Clearing her throat, Evalyn spoke up, "So, are you going to explain what's going on now or are we going to sit in silence a few more minutes?" Evalyn hoped she had not come across as rude, but she was longing for an explanation and she wasn't sure how much patience she had left within her.

The mermaid smiled and rested her tail upon a stool, "What do you desire to know first?"

"Your name would be nice," Adelia answered.

"Aw, my name. Aren't names an amazing curiosity? They describe you, define you. It's your own uniqueness, your own definition," the mermaid seemed deep in thought to Evalyn.

The mermaid continued, "Yes, my calling is Genevieve. I know it's quite curious, it means white wave."

Evalyn didn't quite understand what all Genevieve was explaining, but she spoke anyway, "Well, Genevieve, it is great to finally know your name…"

"Evalyn…" Genevieve interrupted, "Adelia, do you two know what your names mean?"

Evalyn's heart became overwhelmed with a heaviness she could not explain. It was all she could do to look away from Genevieve.

"I assumed not. You see both of your stories are unique. You have two names. One that you are familiar with and have been called all your life, while the other has been locked away and kept from you," Genevieve turned toward Evalyn, "the name that you currently possess is Evalyn which means 'a wished for life'. You were a blessing to whoever raised you. You were a gift, an answer to someone's dreams. Adelia, your name means 'noble'. It is a name that instantly brings you great honor and respect from others around you."

"Wow," Adelia expressed as she leaned in to hear more, "What do you mean by we have another name?"

"You are adopted, aren't you?" Genevieve asked, "Your birth parents named you first. That is your divine and chosen name."

Evalyn felt her body become overwhelmed, "Do you know my name?"

Genevieve shook her head, "That is a question I am not here to answer. Please ask me anything else."

Adelia felt excitement surging through her bones. This mermaid knew so much. *Could she possibly confirm if Evalyn was her twin? Did she know where her parents were?*

"Our parents," Adelia began.

"Aw, so you figured out one piece of the puzzle," Genevieve smiled, "You really are twins."

"I knew it! I knew the shells weren't just a coincidence," Evalyn exclaimed as she touched the specific seashell woven in her hair. Adelia felt her cheeks turn red as she too touched the identical shell in her hair.

"Yes, your mother gave you those on the day you were born. Your mother used to collect shells all the time when she was young," Genevieve explained.

"You knew our mother?" both mergirls whispered.

"How?" Evalyn asked.

Genevieve smiled, "I was her guardian until the day you were born. For that is when I became yours. Now we could sit and talk about the past all day. And we would cry and ache in pain because of it. But we shall not. You must be wondering why you have seemingly aged in years." Neither girl answered Genevieve. Of course, they wanted to know what had transformed them, but more than that, they wanted to know the story about their past. They wanted to hear more about their mother and who their father was.

"Listen, I will explain everything in due time, but we must start with the present," Genevieve spoke, "The moment I felt the surges of your energy sweeping through the ocean years ago, I knew it meant you had found each other…"

"Years ago?" Adelia's heart quickened.

"Let me finish," Genevieve replied, "Your power was so great it brought life to every surviving creature in the Northern Sea Kingdom. The surges have become more powerful in the past two years. I knew you were making your way back to the Northern Sea Kingdom. I suspected that the merman upon the throne had sensed your power as well. And if I wasn't careful, he'd get to you first. But thankfully I did."

"Why did you knock us out?" Evalyn questioned, "The merman upon the throne? Isn't that the King?"

"Not rightfully, but currently, yes the King," Genevieve continued, "I put you asleep because it was not time. You were not of age yet."

"And now we are?" Adelia exclaimed, "How long were we asleep?"

"Five years," Genevieve answered.

"Five years! We're fifteen years old!" Evalyn yelled, "How in the seven seas did you make us sleep for five years."

"Magic of course," Genevieve answered, "You will see much greater things in the next year than you have ever seen before in your life."

Adelia nearly laughed. *How was it possible? She had already seen her own body glow and heal itself. What more could amaze her?*

"I've seen more magic in my whole life since the moment I met Adelia," Evalyn expressed.

"That's true," Adelia added.

"You're magics feed off each other," Genevieve explained, "You two are more connected than any magical being in the ocean. And when you tap into your full power, you will be unstoppable. Oh, I can see it now. The whole family reunited. A true queen and king upon the throne once again!"

Genevieve was beginning to say things that went over Adelia's head, "Does everyone have magic?"

Genevieve laughed, "Everyone possesses a magic that makes them unique and different. Everyone has a power that makes their heart beat in their chest. But darling, your magic is much different and more powerful than any ordinary being. You, my dear, come from royal blood. You possess the power to control the power within you."

Adelia looked at her hands. They seemed ordinary to her.

"Royal… Genevieve, please, tell me who my parents are," Adelia whispered as she continued to stare at the palms of her hands.

⁂

Evalyn felt her body shake with anticipation. *Would this be the moment everything would be explained?*

"Before you were born, the Northern Sea Kingdom was blossoming with life. It was the kingdom that kept the others from entering war. It gave merfolk a place to come for rest and hope. The Northern Sea Kingdom was a unique paradise for outsiders. The kingdoms back then did not care about the color of your tail or your social status. All were welcomed everywhere, mostly because of the work of the Great King and the All Caring Queen of the Northern Sea Kingdom, your grandparents," Genevieve paused slightly, "Your mother and father were young new parents and deeply in love. Their marriage was ideal, and everyone anticipated the day when they too would rule. For your mother was just like her father, the King. She was hardheaded and never gave up on whatever she put her mind to, and your father was musical, full of passion. He was the life of the party."

Evalyn felt her throat closing up and tears threatening to fall from her eyes. *Why was Genevieve speaking in past tense?*

"What happened?" Adelia whispered.

Genevieve's face became serious, "After you were born, an old rotten bandage seemed to have been ripped off a very jealous man in your family's life. He had been pushed to the shadows of your parents and hate had begun to grow within him. He had never been any real kind of trouble."

Genevieve showed her first sign of sadness as she continued to explain, "Everything changed on the day of your mother and father's coronation. The King and Queen had decided that they were ready to pass down the crown. They had served their time, fought their wars, and were ready to enjoy life without all the pressure. They wanted to become fulltime grandparents. On that day, your mother had taken you two and had gone out to prepare her mind for what was about to happen. Your father was studying with the King that day."

Genevieve sighed, "Your father, the King, and the merman in the shadows had gotten into a huge fight an hour before the coronation. I, myself, had heard their words echo through the halls of the castle as I laid your mother's crown upon her dresser. I hadn't thought much about it at the time, because I knew the King would resolve it all. Time went by fast, and you and your mother had not returned. I tried not to worry because your mother was always running late. The King and Queen were all in their places upon the magnificent stage. The whole kingdom was there, cheering in admiration and excitement...." Genevieve lowered her head and a piece of sea glass fell into her lap. Evalyn's heart skipped a beat in her chest as she dreaded what Genevieve was about to say.

"I remember it as if it were yesterday when the King rose to come to speak to me. I assumed he was coming to ask me what the delay was, for your father was waiting right outside the doors of the stage for your mother. I had sent servants out to find her and was waiting for word. He held the Trident high causing the crowd to roar in a thunderous cheer. Then the most unexpected thing that could have ever taken place happened," Genevieve looked as if she were in a trance as she continued to speak, " The merman from the shadows dashed onto the stage and yanked the Trident from the King's hand. A blinding light exploded in the faces of the crowd, but for some reason I could still see. I watched as the King struggled to regain possession of the object that sourced his power. But he had been caught off guard and was unable to regain his ground. The wicked-minded merman thrusted the Trident in the air as what looked like a lightning strike struck through him. His eyes turned white and he let out a possessed laugh of victory. The merman smiled as the King swam backward in fear. He had won. The crowd, still blind, had begun to cry out in fear. At that moment, I remember praying as the King regathered his strength and swam forward on a mission to regain his power back, but it was too late and he was powerless. Next thing I knew, I was watching the trident pierce through the King, killing him instantly. The merman then turned toward my Queen, my darling Queen. The shadow man smiled, just as your father burst through the stage doors, unaware of what was happening. As if in response to the presence of your father, the merman stabbed the Queen in the side killing her on the spot...."

Chills ran up and down Adelia's spine as her past unfolded before her. Never in a million years had she dreamed this would be her story. She had imagined a happy fairytale not a nightmare.

"Your father let out a scream and launched forward," Genevieve continued, "And then ... and then the sapphire at the center of the trident cracked sending a force that created the fiercest hurricane that this planet has ever seen. I was thrown, unconscious, miles out of the kingdom. I must have awoken days later, sore and aching with uncertainty. It took me an entire day to make it back to the Kingdom. And when I got there everything was in devastation. Much like it is now. Not sure what to do, I entered the castle through the servant tunnels. I heard whispers that hinted that there was a new king. Fear overtook me. I snuck into the throne room and to my dismay the dreadful merman was sitting upon the king's throne with the trident in hand. Curiously, the trident looked different. The sapphire stone no longer continuously spun. It was cracked in half. A piece of it was missing and it looked damaged. The new King sat there, laughing and sending servants to do this and that.

I remember my heart pounding as I hurried to Merena's room. She was not there nor was your father in his room. I asked around for information on what had happened to your father and each reply I heard was that he had vanished. I then left the castle, determined to find a way to stop this evil ruler from destroying my home. I knew my only choice was to hide and train in magic myself. I would be no help without the knowledge of magic. So, I learned and waited for your mother to return, but she never did."

Evalyn felt lightheaded as questions beyond even her own comprehension flooded her mind. *Was her mother even alive? What about her father? The mystery merman, who was he? And the stone in the trident, what had happened to it?*

CHAPTER TWENTY-FOUR

The Power of Magic Within

One Day Later

Adelia sat watching the little fish swim in and out of the coral reef. Their life was so simple. They had nothing to worry or fear about, other than to stay alive. Adelia, however, had a much more confusing and complicated life. One moment she was ten years old, dreaming of running into the arms of her waiting parents. Everything would have been perfect, just like the little fishes' lives. There would have been nothing to worry about. And imagine, she would have come home as a princess of a kingdom that would have adored her, yet that wasn't reality. Reality wasn't perfect. Reality was confusing. In reality, she was fifteen and her kingdom was lost. Her mother and father were gone forever? *Was it up to Evalyn and her to save her parents, wherever they were?* Genevieve, after she had explained everything last night, had told the mergirls to get some rest. For the next week or so it was going to be tough until they tapped into their full potential. Genevieve had promised that everything would begin to make more and more sense as the next few days passed. Adelia didn't know what she meant exactly by that but sat in anticipation for what would become of her and Evalyn.

⚜

Evalyn watched Adelia kick her tail up and down against the chair as they both waited for Genevieve to enter the room. Evalyn still felt a heavy weight upon her heart. She dreaded that she would never get to meet her grandparents and she prayed that her parents were still out there. *If not, what would they do? Would it be up to Adelia and her to save the kingdom?*

"My darlings, are you ready to begin our day?" Genevieve asked as she made her way to where the twins were seated, "Well?"

Evalyn looked up as she was ripped from her thoughts, "Of course."

Standing almost instantly with Adelia, Evalyn took a second glance at her twin. *Did she look so grown up, too?* She had yet to see herself in the mirror since when she had lived with the dolphins. It was strange that in her mind that was only a month ago, yet in reality it was over five years ago. *I wonder what Lulu is up to nowadays.*

"Well girls, today we will begin learning more about the strength and power that has been unlocked within you," Genevieve said, "Follow me and listen closely."

Genevieve determinedly swam over to the large golden curtain on the far right of the dining room. She pulled the curtain back revealing another opening.

"It's for safety purposes," Genevieve winked as she swam into the tunnel, "So, like I was saying last night I have been studying magic and the source of it for more than fifteen years since a little bit before you two were born. Magic is a very complex and dangerous thing when not controlled. The two of you combined, when you are at your fullest power, could demolish the entire world. That is why for the next few months I will help you discover and learn to control your power." The deeper the mermaids swam, the more Evalyn began to sense the blood rushing through her veins. She stole a glance back at Adelia to confirm if they were glowing like before. They were, but this time the light was as if it had added one hundred watts.

Evalyn felt queasy, "Why, all of a sudden, do we have power? I think my adopted family would have noticed if I did this when I was younger."

"Like I said, magic is a confusing thing. Only royal mermaids possess true oceanic power. Normal citizens can use magic, like myself; however, unlike yourselves, we are not personally the source of our own magic. It has to come from somewhere else," Genevieve explained, "When a royal mermaid turns sixteen years old, all of the magic barriers within are broken and the magic begins to flow out of them like a rushing river. There are no more restrictions. The four tridents from all four sea kingdoms are the source for all magic. So, it makes sense that the further away you are from your trident, the less power you possess. Especially if your trident happens to be broken or possessed by an evil mad man. At times, you may feel out of control, but that's what I am here for. The reason I believe the two of you are among the most powerful beings in the sea is because of the power you possessed even before you were of age. Imagine what it is going to be like when you can control it. Just imagine." Genevieve squeezed through a tight space between the walls of the tunnel, revealing wide open waters. Nothing but water for miles. Evalyn flinched as her large tail scrapped across the rocks as she too squeezed through into the open water.

"Where are we?" Adelia asked as she joined the two mermaids.

"Miles from anywhere. We are deeper than any human vessel has ever ventured. Their ships tend to become damaged and fail apart a few thousand feet above us," Genevieve spread her arms out, "Here you are free to use your powers without hurting anyone."

Evalyn gave Adelia a questioning look. *How were they supposed to use their powers when they didn't even know how to turn them on and off?*

"Well, let us begin," Genevieve exclaimed, "Tell me what do you think or know you can do?"

"Glow," Evalyn waved her arm at Adelia.

"Yes, your fiery blue hair and striking tails lighting the tunnels and the sea is quite noticeable. Anything else?" Genevieve asked.

"Well, there were the power surges," Adelia said in deep thought, "But I think that's it."

"I healed my own wound when I cut myself in the tunnels," Evalyn added, "But other than that, I think that's all."

"But it isn't," Genevieve expressed, "Your magic is addicting. It makes others want to be with you. Merfolk want what you have even if they don't know what it is. When you were sleeping, I brought sick fish to your room. Within an hour, the breath that you released into the air healed them. The two of you, for an instant, brought this kingdom back to normal. Everyone was healed. There is greatness inside you. We just have to learn how to control it before we release it. And we've got less than a year to do so."

Adelia's face stung as she lifted her head in defeat from the sea floor. Genevieve had had them practicing the same move for an hour now. It was simple in theory, yet seemingly impossible in reality. Spin three times fast and then slow down the world around you. Adelia buried her head in her arms; she was exhausted. She hadn't been able to complete the move once. Evalyn did. In fact, she did it on her third try. Her body had been spinning like normal, but then all of a sudden, the ocean had responded to her. The water circled her like honey. Her movements were slow and graceful. It was amazing. It was like she had slowed down time itself.

"Perfect, Evalyn!" Genevieve exclaimed as Evalyn created a sphere full of oxygen, "Amazing!"

Adelia sighed and looked down at her hands. She felt useless. It wasn't fair.

"Come on, Adelia," Genevieve reached out her hand, "Try something else. We'll work on that move later." Taking Genevieve's hand, Adelia was determined to be as successful as her twin, who had already moved on to the next training.

"What's next then?" Adelia asked.

"How about creating a spark?" Genevieve exclaimed, "I've read that some great kings were able to call lightning from the heavens. Maybe you have that same spark within you."

"How?" Adelia whispered as she scanned her hands.

"To be honest, in all my studies, I wasn't able to find a description of how the kings did this," Genevieve explained, "Try looking deep inside and pulling it from within you."

Could it be possible? Adelia noticed Evalyn had stopped her studies to watch her. Closing her eyes, Adelia felt the cool water against her skin. She imagined the great kings striking down their enemies to save their kingdom. She counted her heart beats ... *one ... two ... three*...All of a sudden, a surge of energy gushed through her veins as if a river dam had broken. Her body shook violently, yet she felt no pain. She only felt power. Adelia opened her eyes, revealing only two blinding lights. Her hands grasped together with great pressure as the energy inside her collected in the palms of her hands. Slowly, Adelia released her hands. Sparks of electricity danced from her fingers. As her hands separated, fewer blue and white sparks flew. As quickly as they had appeared, they disappeared, leaving Adelia feeling a bit more accomplished.

※

Evalyn rushed to give her twin a hug, "You did it! That was so cool!"

Adelia blushed and glanced back at her hands, "I really did!"

"Great job, girls. You are both doing amazing! We have many, many days ahead of us, but I admire your determination," Genevieve nodded, "Let's move on. Adelia, back to the first move and Evalyn let's see that water sphere again."

Adelia's heart sank slightly. *What if she failed again?* But she would not let herself continue to get her down. She would complete the move and she would do it flawlessly! Calming her heart, Adelia raised her arms out and took a deep breath.

CHAPTER TWENTY-FIVE

One Touch

One Year Later

Water pressed against Adelia's body as she torpedoed through the water. Breathing in, she closed her eyes as she felt the water around her slow. She opened her eyes and watched as the water slowly danced around her. It sparkled and glistened around her like the stars in the sky. She smiled and spread her arms. Adelia felt her power collecting in her fingertips. Pausing for effect, she prepared her fingers. Releasing her breath, she snapped her fingers, sending a force as great as a tsunami rushing through the waters in front of her. Closing her eyes, she formed a lasso from the waters and began to fling it in the air. Around and around it went as she flung herself toward the wild wave she had let loose.

Focusing, Adelia breathed in, freezing time. Slowly, she thrust her lasso at the frozen wave. The lasso expanded until it had wrapped itself around the great wave. Pulling tight and securing the lasso around the water, Adelia thrust the energy source back towards her, lessening its power with each tug.

As the wave disappeared, Adelia sighed and whipped the lasso in the air, "That's how it's done! We are so ready for what's to come!"

"You're never ready, trust me," Genevieve replied.

"She's right," Evalyn replied, "But good job anyway."

"In all seriousness, girls. It's time I show you your next steps," Genevieve waved the twins toward the secret entrance to the tunnels. Evalyn gave Adelia a questioning look, but Adelia just shrugged. *Who knew what Genevieve had up her sleeve?*

Genevieve led the girls through the grand dining room and back to the room where they had first arrived. Chills ran down Evalyn's spine as she realized she had lived five of her years transforming into a young woman asleep and hiding in this very room. Evalyn glanced at the hole where Adelia and her had first fallen through. Genevieve guided the twins through a small hole that narrowed slightly upward. Evalyn had never noticed it before. She had to use almost all her strength to pull herself through the entrance, for the water draft was pushing them downward. The tunnel continued upward for a good minute and, as she often did, Evalyn wondered what the Northern Sea Kingdom looked like now. *Was it in complete devastation?*

Evalyn pressed her fins against the rocks of the tunnel to give one more push before releasing herself into a dark room. Genevieve stood still as Adelia joined Evalyn's side.

"There's no light in here, so if you will please fix that, I would be grateful," Genevieve requested as a serious look controlled her face. Evalyn closed her eyes. Gathering herself, she let out a deep breath, releasing a glow from within her. Adelia's tail, hair, skin, and eyes emitted the same blue light as Evalyn, revealing an empty square-shaped room.

"Where are we?" Adelia asked.

"Silence is your friend right now, girls," Genevieve turned toward the far wall of the room, "Today we are going to find some answers." Questions flooded Evalyn's brain as she watched Genevieve raise her arms in preparation. Fighting to hold her tongue, Evalyn studied Genevieve's movements. Her arms gracefully danced in the water, yet no magical spark released from her.

Genevieve's eyes glowed solid white as she turned to the twins, "Take my hand." An energy surged through Evalyn as she grasped the outstretched hand of her guardian. A bright light exploded before her as she stood tall next to Genevieve. She was not afraid, yet her body trembled in awe. The waters around the three mermaids began to spin, rushing in between them. Evalyn knew the power of the waters should have tossed and turned them into the current, but it did not. She felt as if she was feeding from its strength. The power within her seemed to grow; it was like she had become unstoppable.

"Show them what has left an empty hole in their hearts. Show them the thing they long for the most," Genevieve yelled through the rushing sounds of water. Evalyn's mind immediately thought of her mother and father. The blinding light shone with full force as Evalyn closed her eyes in reaction to it. Instantly her mind was filled with memories that weren't hers. A queen, a massive door, thorns, a glowing sceptre, pirates, letters, inscribed words: *The Siphon*, an island, gold coins and jewels, thick bars of a cage, tally marks, and a pile of mermaid sea glass. Emotions hit Evalyn like a raging tsunami. Emptiness, hopelessness, and fear erupted within her. She felt tears gushing through her as she sank to the ocean floor.

Adelia sat rocking herself back and forth. She did not understand the feelings that had so suddenly taken over her. She had seen a vision of a trident. It was as if she had been leaping for it, but as she saw herself nearing the stone at the center, everything vanished. And her body began to ache with loneliness and uncertainty. Her body felt numb and unmovable. Trapped. Somehow forcing her body to calm down as she opened her eyes, Adelia was met with a curious Genevieve who stood patiently waiting for one of the twins to reveal what had happened. Glancing toward Evalyn, Adelia was glad to see that Evalyn was also lying upon the floor in absolute shock.

"Girls," Genevieve spoke, silencing the last bit of unsteady water, "What you have just seen are the clues to finding your parents. So please, when you're ready, tell me everything you felt and saw."

Evalyn sat in awe as Adelia finished telling her vision. They had had completely different experiences, yet Evalyn felt as if she had been beside Adelia experiencing it along with her. Evalyn had already expressed her encounter with the memories.

"Girls, I think you both just saw the memories of your parents," Genevieve joined them on the ground, "Adelia's were your father's. I still don't understand what is happening with him in the memories, but I believe it's safe to say that he's alive. You didn't necessarily experience his death."

Genevieve closed her eyes, "*The Siphon*... Now, Evalyn your stories are a bit more detailed. One thing that stood out to me was *The Siphon*. To me that sounds like a ship, and you said pirates and bars and a cage. I'm afraid that your mother has been captured by pirates of some sort."

"Well, what can we do?" Evalyn blurted out.

"You two are going to go save her, of course," Genevieve expressed.

Adelia frowned, "But how? We don't even know where this pirate ship is."

"But you have a connection to your mother that will lead you to her," Genevieve explained.

"Well, if that was all we needed then why haven't we found her sooner?" Evalyn questioned.

"You've never used all your powers in the correct way for your mother before," Genevieve said plainly. Evalyn shook her head in frustration. *This made no sense.*

"I know you're overwhelmed, but hear me out... You did not possess enough power or mental strength a year ago for a task so draining as the one you are about to embark on," Genevieve's soothing voice filled the room, "In a moment, you will leave me and you will not return without your mother."

The mergirls leaned in, soaking up every word that was released from Genevieve's mouth, "I don't know what you will face nor do I know what you will find when you do get to her. But I have faith you will be successful."

"Why aren't you coming?" Adelia asked.

Genevieve shook her head, "I dare not go, for the waters did not choose this as my destiny. It is not my place, it is yours."

"What about our father?" Evalyn questioned.

"We will find him too, but we can only do so much at one time," Genevieve signaled the twins to rise up, "Take the shells your mother gave you when you were young." Evalyn slowly unbraided the shell from her hair as her heart began to race.

"Now, hold hands, close your eyes, and think about your mother," Genevieve said as she swam toward the exit of the room. The harmonic voice of Genevieve filled Evalyn's ear as it became distant. *La la la la la ... the song,* Evalyn thought. The one that Adelia had been singing when they had first met. Evalyn's body began to tremble as the shell in her hand burned like fire. She imagined the fiery spirit of her mother and the strength that she must have possessed to stay alive all these years. Evalyn felt her body go numb. Her eyes became heavy as she listened to the lovely tone of the song that seemed to bounce off the walls of the cave. *Everything felt so close to being the life she had hoped and dreamed for*, Evalyn thought as she drifted off into a deep sleep.

Crashing waves filled Adelia's mind as she slowly began to awaken from her slumber. Her muscles ached as she felt unsteady water threaten to drift her far away. Her eyes opened suddenly to a chaotic scene. Large dark waves crashed before her eyes, filling her head with thunderous sounds. Yet she only felt the mere ripple of the great, powerful waves. Glancing around, she noticed Evalyn staring in amazement at the horrific storm. Strangely, the waters around the two mergirls were calm.

All of a sudden, Adelia felt her tail begin to be pulled in toward the storm. Uncertainty swept over her as she struggled to keep from being swept away in the underwater current.

"Adelia!" Evalyn's eyes met Adelia's, revealing the fear within them both, "Look!"

Glancing forward, Adelia froze. A monstrous wave was gathering up before them, threatening to destroy everything in its path.

Grasping Evalyn's hand, Adelia yelled, "Let's get out of here!" Turning suddenly, Adelia nearly screamed as she slammed face first into wooden planks. The waves began to beat against her body. *I must have left the safe zone.* Still holding Evalyn's hand, with all her might, Adelia grasped the side of the mysterious wooden planks. *What was she supposed to do now?*

Closing her eyes, Evalyn let out a deep breath. She had to focus on her mother. That was the only way Adelia and she were going to make it out of this alive. She imagined her mother grasping her tightly and assuring her everything was going to turn out all right. She imagined how her mother would glow with beauty. How the sound of saying her own mother's name would be like singing a song to the heavens. Evalyn relaxed as she felt her body lift from the waves. Her grip tightened with Adelia's as a gust of wind pounded her body. She opened her eyes to reveal that it wasn't just wooden planks they had been pushed against, but a pirate ship. Evalyn gasped as a bright light burst from her tail. Spiraling down toward the surface of the giant vessel, Evalyn watched as her tail began to disappear. And quicker than she could say the word megalodon, her fin transformed into two legs clothed in jeans shorts. She wasn't fearful, but curious. The tank top upon her chest made her wonder how strange she must look.

Evalyn's eyes grew as her new legs touched the floor of the ship. *This must be The Siphon.* Strength fueled through her body as she stood tall. Pirates were running around, throwing out water and crying for help. *They must fear the colossal wave forming in the distance.* The twins seemed unnoticed as they walked past the fearful pirates. *Was it merely the danger of the approaching wave that kept the mergirls from being seen or was Adelia doing some kind of magic that made them invisible to the naked eye?*

"What now?" Evalyn whispered.

"We find our mother," Adelia answered, "Wanna split…"

Evalyn interrupted, "No … I think we should stay together."

Adelia nodded, "Look…"

Evalyn followed Adelia's finger to an elegantly looking woman as she unlocked a door in the floor.

"Let's follow her," Adelia said as she slowly began pursuit with her newly acquired legs.

Merena's body shook. Her eyes felt as if they were going to burst from her face. Her stomach pained with each faint heartbeat. An overwhelming fear struck as she heard the all too familiar sound of the clopping of heels. *How long had it been since Queen Ramona had visited?* Merena had lost count. She dreaded the nearing moments. For if Queen Ramona was right, then these would be her last.

"Ah, Merena," Queen Ramona sang out, "I've waited too long for this day." The sceptre within Queen Ramona's grasp shone with twice the magnitude than it had before. Merena's body and soul longed to hold it. Part of her felt that if she could just touch it then she would regain her strength and once beloved power.

An unlocking of chains filled her ears, "Merena, today is special. Do you know why?"

Merena didn't move and for an instant she thought she heard the sound of more footsteps. Probably James and Jaxson.

Queen Ramona circled around Merena, "Boy, you're a sight for sore eyes, my dear. Now tell me, do you want to feel some of my power?"

Merena knew she shouldn't but her pounding head was so desperate for something to relieve the pounding thirst surging through her body and soul that she shook her head yes.

"Then touch the sapphire," Queen Ramona hung the sceptre in front of Merena's eyes. Merena lifted her shaking hand. *What else was she to do? Maybe she could fight whatever evil may enter her? She could use it for good.* Just as her hand touched the broken sapphire, she heard a petrified scream. But it was too late. For there was a flash of light just before darkness invaded her vision. She saw nothing, then felt nothing, then was nothing.

❈

Adelia braced herself as a huge force sent her crashing into and through the walls of the pirate ship. She screamed as broken pieces of wood stabbed her every which way. A gust of fresh air shocked her as she continued to be thrown backward. She gasped as her body flung through the open air and crashed into the ocean. The force of impact nearly knocked her out.

Gasping for air, Evalyn feared that she had been flung miles from the ship. Questions raced through her mind faster than she could comprehend. *Was she lost from all she loved, again? Had that been her mother in the jail? Who was that mysterious woman? Why had all those girls been caged in that ship?* Taking a deep breath, Evalyn felt a little relieved that within the time she had been flung from the boat to the water her tail had returned. She scanned the sea to see what looked like the remains of a shipwreck. Diving into the sea, Evalyn glanced around in confusion. There was a massive number of conch shells that were floating to the bottom of the sea floor. *Perhaps it was only her imagination.* Evalyn followed the broken pieces of wood toward the surface.

As her head broke the barrier of the water, she heard cheers and laughter. Scanning the waters, Evalyn was surprised to find that the storms had subsided and a group of diverse mermaids and mermen had gathered in the middle of the debris. Rushing towards the group, Evalyn hoped to find her long lost mother amongst them.

CHAPTER TWENTY-SIX

An Old Friend

A dim light caught Adelia's eye as she scanned the waters beneath her. Curious, she neared the glowing light in the sand. An elaborate, thorn-infested stick stuck out from the sea floor. Slowly and carefully Adelia pulled it out of the sand, revealing a sapphire at the end. As Adelia studied it she felt a source of power billow up within her. It seemed to be in sync with her heartbeat. Adelia felt as if the emptiness inside her was being filled up. All those nights she had spent alone seemed to not matter.

"I have to show Evalyn. Maybe this is our next clue," Adelia whispered as she headed toward the surface.

As her head broke through the waters, Adelia was shocked to see Evalyn wandering through a crowd of mermaids and mermen. *What all had she missed?*

Just as Adelia was about to call out for Evalyn, her eyes caught sight of a familiar looking mermaid. Adelia's heart skipped, "It couldn't be... Tiera! Tiera!" Adelia raced as fast as she could to the mermaid whose back was turned. *The blond hair, the glistening tail. It just had to be her.*

"Tiera!" Adelia nearly ran into the young mermaid.

The mermaid turned around to see many other mermaids staring, "Yes?"

Adelia waited, *would she recognize her?*

"Wait … Adelia, is that you?" Tiera grasped Adelia in her arms, "I was afraid I'd never see you again! Were you captured this whole time?"

"No, I've been … well, it's a long story," Adelia nodded at Evalyn who had made her way beside Adelia.

Tiera gasped, "You have a twin?"

Adelia smiled, "Yes, and there's a lot more than that."

"What's that?" Evalyn questioned as she noticed the sceptre in Adelia's hand.

Tiera's eyes grew wide and so did many of the other mermaids around them as they too noticed the sceptre.

"Adelia, that's Queen Ramona's sceptre," Tiera whispered.

"Queen Ramona who?" Adelia asked.

Tiera nodded, "She's the one that turned us into her slaves. She would touch our skin with a conch shell and then I guess the power within us was transferred into that sceptre. But you can see that we have no mark on our skin anymore. We're free!"

"You've been caged up this whole time?" Evalyn sighed.

Tiera nodded, "Yeah we have. It really helped me realize something, though. Even though all of us come from different places, we all are still struggling with the same challenges. Fear, time, loneliness, and the need to be loved."

"What are you going to do now that you're free?" Adelia asked.

"Go home," Tiera explained, sending the rest of the mermaids into celebration, "I want to help all the Kingdoms realize it doesn't matter where you're from. Everyone can be friends, and everyone can be family." Tiera grabbed hold of a tall, handsome, eastern merman.

"Who's this?" Adelia's eyes sparkled with mischief.

Tiera blushed and looked into the hazel eyes of the merman, "This is Narayan from the Eastern Sea Kingdom."

"It's nice to meet you, Narayan," Adelia replied, giving Tiera a wink.

"So, will you be coming home with us?" Tiera asked.

"I can't. The kingdoms are at war, Tiera. I fear I won't be able to see your mother until after the drift between the kingdoms has been healed," Adelia sighed as Tiera's face looked crushed. The merfolk around the twins had begun to whisper in fear.

"Where will you go?" Tiera questioned.

Evalyn waved her arm around, "As you can see, we are the only mermaids from the Northern Sea Kingdom here. You all will be saved as long as you return to your kingdoms soon. I do not know when the war is going to become deadly or if it even will. Let's hope for the best."

"Evalyn and I must find our parents in order to take back the Northern Sea Kingdom," Adelia explained, "Our parents are the rightful heirs. That monster who sits upon the throne today is definitely not."

"You are royalty?" Tiera gasped, "I had no clue!"

"Us either," Evalyn answered. The sun continued to escape behind the horizon and darkness was slowly creeping in.

"We better get going soon," a Southern mermaid spoke.

An Eastern mermaid nodded, "Shall we travel by kingdom?" Many mermaids spoke out in agreement and began to create three groups. Adelia noticed that a few were mixing in with different groups of their origin. A new reality was beginning to form and Adelia was sure she was going to love it.

"Tiera, I'm going to miss you," Adelia sighed.

"We will see each other again. You have to promise to come to visit the Southern Sea Kingdom once you're back to your regular princess duties," Tiera smiled.

Adelia laughed, "I will. Tell your mother that I found you and that I'm so sorry for everything." Tiera nodded and turned to join Narayan and the southern merfolk.

"Bye!" Adelia exclaimed as she watched the tail of her adopted sister disappear beneath the waves.

※

Evalyn noticed the sad look in Adelia's eyes. It made her wonder where Lulu was right now. *Had she been drafted into one of the armies? Had she even survived for the past, what was it? Six years?*

Adelia rolled the sceptre in her hand, "Let's get back to Genevieve. Mom's not here nor is the woman who was in the cage, that mysterious woman, and the pirates. They are gone, vanished into thin air. We just gotta show Genevieve this. Maybe she will understand what happened here."

Evalyn nodded as she looked at the debris of the wrecked ship. It was the only thing left behind. *Where had all the pirates gone? That woman? And the prisoner?* "You ready?" Adelia asked as she grabbed Evalyn's hand. "I'm ready," Evalyn sighed as she closed her eyes and began to hum. She felt the similar deep sleep settle within her. The water felt like a cozy blanket as she once again fell into a deep slumber.

Adelia opened her eyes to the familiar dining room of Genevieve's cave. She sighed in relief at not only the sight of Evalyn, but also the sceptre. Part of her had feared it would not make the trip.

"Girls!" Genevieve rushed into the room, "You made it back. Where's your mother?"

Evalyn sighed, "We may have seen her. We aren't sure what happened exactly, but we helped free quite a few merfolk."

"And we found this!" Adelia lifted the sceptre up for Genevieve to see.

"I noticed," Genevieve studied the sapphire upon the sceptre, "Interesting."

Out of nowhere, Genevieve let out a gasp, "Look at that!" She pointed at the sharp, broken edges of the sapphire, "It's not complete! Could it be?"

"Could it be what?" Adelia felt excitement rush through her veins.

Genevieve nodded, "Girls, you've gotten your hands on one of the broken pieces of the sapphire that belongs inside the trident. This explains why the current King hasn't been able to destroy the entire ocean yet. He hasn't had access to the trident's full power."

"I've got a question," Adelia spoke up, "You may have said this already and I may have just not been listening, but who is the King exactly?"

Genevieve nodded, "I've been waiting for one of you to ask me. He's your uncle, your mother's brother."

"Oh…That explains why he's got magic," Adelia nodded connecting more dots to the giant mystery inside her head.

"Precisely," Genevieve responded.

"Well, what are we supposed to do now?" Evalyn questioned.

Genevieve motioned toward the dining room table, "Tell me every bit of detail you remember from your quest. Then we will decide our next path to take."

Tiera's heart dropped as her eyes saw the gates of the Southern Sea Kingdom; it was split in two. Smoke rose from the sides, which she assumed had previously been set on fire.

"My home," Tiera whispered.

"I am so sorry," Narayan pulled her in close.

Slowly, Tiera advanced with the other previously-captured merfolk. No one spoke another word, for the scene before them said it all. As Tiera entered through the gates, a chill ran down her spine as she realized that the rest of the kingdom matched the fate of the gate. Stores and houses were falling to pieces as Tiera stood in shock. Her heart skipped a beat as she realized that the usually busy streets were now eerily empty. *Why had the twins not told her of the status of her kingdom? Maybe they did not know.* Tiera made her way through the streets toward her home. Mourning cries filled her ears as Tiera noticed movement in the windows of the few still standing homes. *How long had it been like this?* Turning onto her street, Tiera was met with a wailing that pierced her heart. The last hundred yards to her house were like swimming through murky water. She hung closer to the Narayan's side. The warmth from his muscles calmed her fear of what she might meet up ahead.

Everything around her faded away when she caught sight of her home. It was damaged, but not to the point where it was unrecognizable. As Tiera swam up to the front entrance, she realized the cries she had been hearing were coming from inside.

"Stay here... Let me go in first," Tiera told Narayan. He simply nodded and watched her go straight in, for the door had been broken down. The walls of the home were burnt black and it seemed that every foot a panel in the floor had been pulled out. Turning into the kitchen, Tiera's heart relaxed as she saw her Mom, head in arms. Her cries pained Tiera as she approached, silently.

"Mom," Tiera whispered.

Her Mom's head slowly rose from the table. Her eyes filled with tears as she scanned Tiera in uttermost shock.

"You are dead," her Mother whispered.

Tiera felt as if her heart would pound out of her chest, "No, I had been captured, but I'm free now. Thanks to Adelia."

"She's alive too?" her mother shook her head, "She cannot be here."

"She is not here and she is safe, but that's a story for another time. What happened here?" Tiera slid into the seat next to her mother.

"The Northern Sea Kingdom..." her mother choked, "Only a week ago, your father had said that the Northern Sea Kingdom was a joke. I mean all these months of a so-called war and we haven't even needed to move a muscle. We let our guard down and that's exactly what the Northern Sea Kingdom wanted." Chills ran down Tiera's spine as her mother stared off into the distance.

"Then two days ago, the sound of a great trumpet filled everyone's ears. And within minutes, the Northern Army broke the barriers and stormed the city," tears streamed down Tiera's mother's face, "They set everything ablaze, killing anyone in their path... I was at home making dinner. Your father was commanding the front lines... Oh Tiera, he did not make it." It was as if a tsunami had hit Tiera. Her mind flooded with so many questions that she couldn't think.

"When the warning siren began to pierce my ears and I heard cries in the streets, I hid in Adelia's room. I waited for your sisters to come home and prayed. Oh, how I prayed," Tiera's mother placed her hand on Tiera, "They didn't come home either. I thought I had lost everyone. I know that God returned you to me because I don't think I could have lived without you." *I didn't even get to say goodbye. I didn't even get to say I love you.*

Tiera laid her head upon her mother's lap. *Oh, how she had missed the comfort of her mother.* She wanted to speak, to tell her mother how much she had missed her, yet all she did was cry.

"We are going to be ok," Tiera's mother whispered.

Evalyn sighed, Genevieve always had the most delicious food prepared.

"This is all very interesting. So, the pirates, the mystery woman, and your mother just disappeared? Adelia, let me see the sceptre for a moment," Genevieve motioned as Adelia handed the sceptre across the table.

Genevieve's eyes grew larger with each passing moment as she studied the sceptre. She turned it every which way and felt in between every engraved detail.

"It just can't be," Genevieve whispered.

Evalyn was beginning to become impatient, "What can't be? What is it?"

"This sapphire here," Genevieve pointed, "It looks broken. Like a piece is missing."

"It does," Adelia exclaimed.

Evalyn nearly shot from her seat in excitement as the light bulb went off, "It's gotta be the other half of the trident's sapphire. It had to have broken when my father touched it."

"You both said there was a bright light and a force, just like what I described when your father touched the trident. That's no mere coincidence," Genevieve stood and began to pass the sceptre back to Adelia.

"What happens when the stone is put back together?" Adelia questioned.

"Right now, the King hasn't been able to control the entirety of the ocean because he hasn't had full power. When the stone is put back together, its full power will be released. Make sense?" Genevieve explained.

"And we don't want the King to be the one holding the trident when it does," Evalyn was nodding. This was all starting to make sense, except for all the disappearing women and pirates.

"What now…" Adelia began to speak but a loud stomping filled the room. Evalyn grabbed onto one of the dining room chairs as the room began to shake.

"What is that?" Evalyn exclaimed as pieces of rock began to crumble to the sand floor.

Genevieve motioned them toward the exit, "It sounds like the footsteps of an army! Let's get out of here!" Hurrying to stay with Genevieve, Evalyn tried to stay calm. At the moment, no large rocks had dislodged. However, if the army continued to pound their tails upon the surface above them, it was highly possible the cave would crash down around them at any moment. The pounding was a technique used to send a warning to an opponent. It was supposed to strike fear into the enemy. And for Evalyn, it was working.

CHAPTER TWENTY-SEVEN

The King

Adelia took a deep breath as the three mermaids exited the hidden cave. She wondered if the few other beings she had seen working for Genevieve had made it out. Adelia followed Genevieve and Evalyn into a bed of seaweed. The ground still shook and the waves were unsteady as the advancing army marched nearby.

"Do you see them?" Adelia questioned.

Genevieve nodded, "They are heading back from what looks like a victory in the South."

"The Southern Sea Kingdom? That's where I grew up. What do you think happened?" Adelia exclaimed, nearly out of breath. *Was Tiera safe? What if she had run into the army on her way home?*

"What are we supposed to do now?" Evalyn asked as she took the sceptre from Genevieve, "What if we used this somehow? Aren't we as powerful as that King now?"

Genevieve stared off into the distance, "Stronger perhaps, but less experienced. We've got to play the longer and smarter game."

"Ok, tell us what to do and we will do it," Adelia nodded.

"I will, but first I must show you one more thing to complete your training," Genevieve motioned toward the seafloor, "Stay low to the ground, we are going into the city."

Adelia nodded. *What else did they have to learn? Didn't they just free a bunch of captured mermaids from bloodthirsty pirates? True, they didn't technically complete the mission .... and come back with their mother and live happily ever after, but at least they got this sceptre thing, right?* Adelia's mind wondered as she swam in line with Genevieve and Evalyn. They were heading into yet another secret cave-like tunnel. Excitement filled her veins as they approached another cave entrance. The last time she had been in the city of her birthplace, it had been only for a minute, and back then she was merely a lonely child. Now she had a bond with her sister that not even magic could break. And there was also the fact that she was literally magical now.

❈

Evalyn felt the sadness of the rocks in the cave they had entered. The rocks were worn and poorly kept, with sharp rigid parts. She could feel them calling out for help. Evalyn tried to see in front of Genevieve as she squeezed through a medium-sized opening. Evalyn easily followed for she had no problem fitting through.

She heard Adelia gasp as she arrived beside her. In front of them was a dark street full of merfolk, sick ones, dirty ones, starving ones. The street was absent of all life or hope. Chills ran down Evalyn's back as she slowly moved down the street. A young mother was rocking her barely clothed baby to sleep as three teenagers were beating each other to death beside her.

A tug at her tail caused Evalyn to turn around. She met the eyes of a hopeless child. It did not speak; it only rubbed its tummy. Evalyn's insides tore, she wanted to give the child something to eat. In fact, she wanted to feed everyone on this street. Glancing behind the child, Evalyn saw a mother, who seemed to be only bones, lean to kiss the forehead of her weakened husband. He seemed to cough every time he lifted his head to take a breath. The woman simply nodded for Evalyn to keep moving. Evalyn felt an anger growing in her stomach. *How could someone let these merfolk starve to death? How could that cruel King upon the throne sit back and watch as his kingdom suffered?*

Turning, Evalyn heard whispers beginning to rise around her. *Is that our Queen? She's back? No, it can't be, there's two of them? Plus, she would have aged.*

Evalyn glanced down at her hands. Could she create enough food to feed these people? Evalyn looked up at Genevieve, who merely shook her head no. Just as Evalyn was about to ball her hands in anger, Adelia's cold hand grasped Evalyn's and pulled her toward Genevieve who had turned down an empty alley.

"This is our kingdom, Evalyn. These are our people," Adelia whispered. She was right. They were the rightful heirs to the throne. Not that coward of a king.

Evalyn frowned, "I will do anything to save these people, Genevieve, what must we do?"

Genevieve smiled, raised her hands in the air, and snapped her fingers, "If you are in trouble I will send help, but I believe you're ready."

※

Darkness invaded Adelia's mind as she held tightly to Evalyn's grasp. She felt rushing water circle them with great force.

However, she did not feel afraid. She felt powerful, she felt safe, and she felt ready for whatever she was about to face.

The King laughed with joy as he felt the unsteadiness of the waters. He sat high upon his throne bathing in his own success. At this very moment, he had seized control of the Southern Sea Kingdom, was attacking the Eastern Sea Kingdom, and had troops preparing to attack the Western Sea Kingdom. Everything was falling into place. He had nothing to worry about. Well, nothing except for the few missing puzzle pieces to his plan. Mysteries like the location of the other half of the trident's sapphire and the mysterious set of twins who kept reappearing every once in a while, and the fact that no one ever saw Merena die. In fact, that was a part of his plan that happened without his doing. She was supposed to die the same way as her parents, but she never returned. Her husband, on the other hand was no longer an issue after his brave attempt to take the trident. It failed obviously. The King only assumed he had vanished into thin air, evaporated, or something mystical like that. Once again, he wasn't exactly sure where Merena's husband had gone, but he hadn't bothered him yet. So the King didn't care.

A strong pull of the waters caught the King's attention, "What in the world?"

A mini whirlpool formed within ten feet of the King. He tightened his grip as the waters threatened to pull him. Seconds passed as he promised himself that he would make whoever was responsible for his discomfort pay. He watched as the waves subsided leaving two identical northern mermaids.

Anger surged through the King's veins as he stared at the mermaids before him. They were oddly familiar and outright breathtaking. The King observed the way their faces glowed with determination and strength. And their tails and hair seemed to literally emit a sapphire blue glow.

Gripping his trident, the King stood, "Who do you think you are to enter my throne room without being summoned. I should kill you now."

"We should kill you for being in our throne room without being summoned," the mermaid on the left said with great authority.

"Of course, we are generous and forgiving," the other one said, just as determined. The King growled in frustration. *Who did these mergirls think they were to come bursting into his kingdom like this?*

"Who are you?" the King tightened his grip. Fear swirled in his stomach as he anticipated their answers. *Why could he never do anything without his older sister involving herself in it?*

The mermaids raised their hands closest to each other and for the first time the King noticed that they were holding a sceptre. The King felt a wave of triumph race up his spin. This was not just a sceptre. *These fools. They've brought me the other half the sapphire stone.* All he had to do was take the sceptre and he would become the most powerful and evil being in the seas. All he had to do was swipe it from the little mermaids. The King smiled, to him it did not matter if he had to kill another life to do so, for these mergirls were just a little bump on his road to success.

✳

Evalyn hoped her shaking body was not noticeable to the King. *Why had Genevieve just thrown them into this? Couldn't she have given them some kind of warning?* His mere image made Evalyn want to turn away and hide. He was huge, a beast. His muscles rippled as he glared at Evalyn and Adelia. Evalyn feared he could see straight into her soul.

"I am Princess Adelia of the Northern Sea Kingdom, daughter of the rightful heirs to this kingdom," Adelia spoke loud and clear.

"And I am Princess Evalyn of the Northern Sea Kingdom, granddaughter of the King and Queen you murdered," Evalyn forced herself to sound as brave as Adelia. This was what they had trained for. She had to focus and remember all the magic tricks within her. She had to remember who this was for.

Adelia watched as anger continued to grow inside the King as he approached the two mermaids. Adelia closed her eyes and breathed, everything was going ok so far. Genevieve had told them that they performed better when they were improving. *I guess that's what she thought would be best to do here.* Adelia focused on the water between herself and the King. It slowed and became like quicksand.

The King struggled for a moment, but then let out a laugh, "You think that will stop me? You don't even know who you really are. Why should that threaten me?" And with a wave of a hand, the King returned the water to normal. He winked.

Adelia gasped as her body went numb. Genevieve had said that she had another name. The one she was born with. She watched her body begin to shake out of control. The King came closer and brushed the hair out of her face. He was saying something, but Adelia could not hear him. *He's probably telling us his evil plan. The villains in her books always did that before they actually tried to do something evil. Why? Adelia wasn't really sure. It honestly made no sense.*

Fear began to overtake Adelia. It came like a rushing wave, but she forced herself to stay calm. Closing her eyes, she focused on getting help. She focused on the only merfolk she could think of that would risk their lives for her. She only hoped they were still alive.

CHAPTER TWENTY-EIGHT

An Army Like Never Before

"I am so glad to have met you, Narayan. Honestly, during another time I don't know what I would have thought. You're from another Kingdom and grew up in a different background and all, but you make Tiera happy and that makes me happy," Tiera's mother said as she, Tiera, and Narayan made their way to the Southern Sea Castle.

They were visiting the general of the army to get information on what exactly had happened on the front lines. Tiera's mother had worked closely with her husband and knew just as much as any merman did when it came to war tactics.

The entire kingdom had been devastated by the battle. Even the castle looked as if it would take months before it would sparkle and shine as it once did. The centuries old, spiraling shells that had once made up the towers of the castle had crumbled. It left a knot in Tiera's throat as they went across the courtyard to where the highest-ranking general was talking up a storm with one of his mersoldiers.

"What do you mean, what are we going to do? We have to strike back!" the general thrust his arms in the air, "This is obviously not a waste of time anymore."

"Sir," the mersoldier stumbled with his words, "Over three-fourths of the army has been eliminated. We are in no shape to fight."

"This is ridiculous, what do you suppose we do?" the general shouted.

"Is it true that you called back a third of the guards because you thought it was a waste of time?" Tiera's mother spoke up, receiving a nasty look from the already-heated general. The general quickly changed his face as he released the one who was speaking.

"Madam, excuse my rudeness. Would you like to join our conversation?" the general motioned her over.

"If you'll answer my question," Tiera's mother huffed as she joined them.

Tiera did not understand much of what they were talking about. She wasn't really into war tactics and battle plans. Tiera grasped the arms of Narayan as a strange feeling swept over her. She glanced at her Mom, who had stopped her conversation to look at Tiera.

"Adelia," her mother mouthed. In that instant, Tiera's world went black as rushing water swarmed over her. She wanted to scream, to grab her mother's or Narayan's hand, but her mind could only think of Adelia. Something was wrong and for some reason she felt like it was her job to fix it.

※

Lulu fought to stay focused as her dolphin troops prepared to battle the Northern army. Her mind had been on Evalyn for days now. However, today she found herself barely able to function. Something was up.

"You ok, Lulu?" one of Lulu's commanders asked.

"I keep thinking of a mergirl named Evalyn," at the mention of Evalyn's name, darkness invaded Lulu's mind. She struggled for a second as water surrounded her. For an instant, she feared for her life, but then her mind fell back to Evalyn. If something was wrong, Lulu promised she would do anything to save her.

Evalyn forced herself to open her eyes. She still could not feel anything as the King lifted her chin. He looked at her with such pity that Evalyn wanted to spit in his face. Hoping her magic had worked, Evalyn watched the King's eye. Seconds later, the King's glance shot behind Evalyn and to the right, then left, and right again. He began to back up. Evalyn smiled as she felt the numbness across her whole body begin to reside. She winced as the all too familiar feeling of her body waking up again swept over her. She always hated when that happened. The stinging sensation was never a wanted feeling. Sound waves began to connect with her ears again, just in time for her to hear the King's reaction.

"Who are you? And you? Dolphins? Is this some kind of joke?" for the first time Evalyn thought she heard fear in the King's voice.

Glancing down, Evalyn was relieved to see that the sceptre was still in their possession. *Why did villains always waste time on talking?* Evalyn's eyes connected with Adelia's. She was grinning as she nodded behind them. Turning, Evalyn was not shocked to see that the entire throne room was filled with a unique-looking army. Dolphins, Southern Sea Kingdom mersoldiers, and mermaids stood glaring at the King.

"Looks like we think alike, too!" Adelia whispered as she turned toward the King.

The King surveyed his throne room with disgust. *How were these invaders appearing in his throne room?* It seemed that with every heartbeat, the number of dolphins and merfolk multiplied. The throne room door began to shake from a pounding on the outside. For the first time in years, fear swept through the King's body as the doors to his throne room burst open. Weak and pathetic citizens of the Northern Sea Kingdom came raging through to join the army created by the twins.

"Down with the King!" the piercing screams of his subjects made him want to kill them all that instant, but if he did he would have no one to rule. Following his betraying citizens were more mersoldiers. But this time they were from the South, East, and West. *How had someone gotten these merfolk to stand together, let alone work together? And where were his guards?*

The King's eyes fell onto a mermaid that was all too familiar to him. A mermaid from his awful past. No wonder she was a part of his downfall. The mermaid locked eyes with him and he nearly struck her dead. *Why did he not?* If he failed because of it, he would curse himself for this weak spot deep within his mind.

The King grinned through his teeth, "Genevieve, why did you betray me? Why did you honor my sister more than me?" The King's eyes darted across the throne room.

"Megalodons protect me!" the King swiped the trident through the air. A large smoke cloud from behind him appeared as an evil grin appeared across his face.

Over a hundred Megalodons, each larger than two blue whales, appeared behind the King. Adelia gasped at the terrifying beasts. Their teeth hung jagged and crooked out of their massive mouths. The eyes of each beast were bright yellow and full of vengeance. Even the smell of their breath caused Adelia's skin to crawl in disgust. Peeking behind her, Adelia looked at her frightened army of misfits. A slight pang of guilt swept over her as she saw Tiera, her mother, and Narayan. *If they die because of this … I'll never be able to forgive myself.* Adelia turned back toward Evalyn as she gathered everyone together.

"Down with the King! Down with the King!" Evalyn chanted as she raised the sceptre in the air. Within seconds, Adelia felt the voices of the merfolk behind her continue to fill the room. The confidence of their army began to rise as the Megalodons continued to grow impatient.

The King raised his trident, preparing to attack.

Grasping the sceptre alongside Evalyn, Adelia glared at the King. There was going to be only one winner at the end of this fight, and he wasn't it!

CHAPTER TWENTY-NINE

The Trident and the Sceptre

At the release of the King's arm, the battle was triggered. Megalodons stormed forward killing any mercreature that unfortunately fell into its path. The King merely stood and watched as the invaders continued to fall. Lulu and the dolphins attacked at full force, taking down as many megalodons as they could. A group of armed mersoldiers circled the twins as they continued to push their way toward the King. Death continued to pile up. It was everywhere.

※

Evalyn tried to stay calm as she watched her best friend and adopted mother fall to the ground. *Lulu!* Rage surged through Evalyn's veins. She would not let this terrible King get away with this. Megalodons crashed every few feet in defeat, summoning the waters this way and that. Adelia and Evalyn were only a few feet away from the King now. Evalyn could feel the power of the sceptre pulling her closer. Adelia had made a bubble somewhat like a force field around them. The armed mermaids that had been around the twins had already given their lives to the cause. Evalyn tried to keep guilt and sadness from distracting her from their mission. The twins assumed the King had created a force field around himself as well, since he wasn't being impacted by anything on his high and mighty throne.

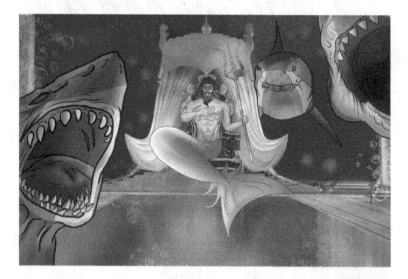

A massive megalodon swam inches above the twins' heads as they crept behind the throne of the King unnoticed. Adelia nodded for Evalyn to let go of the sceptre. Forcing herself to watch, Evalyn took a deep breath as Adelia swam to the upper left side of the throne where the King was holding the trident. Slowly, Adelia glanced over the side of the throne. At any other time, Evalyn would have been amused by how she and Adelia were practically reading each other's minds. *It could have been just them working together, but Evalyn had a feeling*

magic had something to do with it too. Evalyn's heart raced as she stood watching and Adelia began to reach for the trident.

Adelia said a slight prayer as she watched the King rest the trident on its built-in stand. *How could he be so relaxed when there was a literal battle happening in his own throne room?* Taking a deep breath, Adelia closed her eyes. Reality slapped her like a gushing wave. *I better have my eyes open for this. Ok, on the count of three I am just going to grab it and swing over the back of the throne. One, two, three.*

Energy surged through Adelia as she grabbed the trident. Not realizing her own strength, the trident easily slipped out of its stand and to the back of the throne. Quickly, Adelia pointed the trident at the sceptre, just as Evalyn aimed the sceptre at the trident.

The King let out a piercing scream as the trident disappeared from his sight. Swirling around to the back of his throne, he watched as the tips of the trident and the sceptre touched. *How had these merkids outsmarted him? Oh, how he had underestimated their intelligence. How could he have been so stupid?* A light brighter than the sun filled the King's eyes. A power of a thousand tsunamis quickly followed. The King lost control of his body as the power tossed him through the waters. *Bang!* The pain of a shark bite filled his head. His blood seemed to escape faster than he could produce it. *Had his head hit a stone? Or a wall?* He tried to sit up, but his head felt woozy and throbbed unbearably. His heart pounded against his chest, threatening to explode. He felt his body give up as the waves continued to crash upon him. *How had his reign slipped from his fingers so fast?* His petty dreams of ruling the entire seas as one Kingdom vanished. *All those nights plotting against his sister and his ugly brother wasted… No! Destroyed by two meaningless mermaids.* The tempting feeling of sleep swept over the King. He let out one final breath before drifting into the forbidden eternal sleep of a defeated king.

CHAPTER THIRTY

Broken Shells Restored

Merena took in a giant breath as her body awoke once again. Her tail stung as the blood flow rushed back into it. *Wait, her tail?* Excitement rushed through Merena's veins. *What had happened after she reached for the sceptre? Hadn't she blacked out?* Slowly opening her eyes, Merena was met with the most confusing sight. There was death and destruction all around her, in *her* throne room. Megalodons, merfolk … and pirates lay on the ground in defeat. There were exhausted Southern, Western, and Eastern Kingdom soldiers standing in victory around the defeated bodies. *What were they doing here?*

Merena gasped as she saw Queen Ramona's body on the seafloor. A chill engulfed Merena. Queen Ramona had drowned along with the pirate crew. She looked dead, *very* dead. Yet, her dress and skin did not bear a single scratch or tear. To Merena, she looked almost peaceful. For a second, Merena wondered what the human world would do without Queen Ramona… *Who was she kidding, the mermaids would be free and the humans would most likely be celebrating?*

Merena pulled her hand to her mouth in shock. *Tiberius, my brother.* Merena felt a tear roll down her cheek as she turned away from the death scene of her younger brother. It was too much for her to bear. Merena knew that he was the only one who could have caused all the devastation around her. She had feared all along that this was the truth. *Why had he hated her so much? Why had he always done the wrong thing? Why couldn't he have been good?* Merena's heart ached as she blamed herself. *I should have done something to help him to the good in life more. If I had been here, maybe I could have stopped him.*

Glancing at the palms of her hands, Merena let out a deep breath that she hadn't realized she had been holding in. The mark of Queen Ramona that had been permanently scarred on her was gone. She no longer belonged to Queen Ramona; she was free. Merena rubbed her fingers against the locket that still lay upon her chest since the beginning of her time with Queen Ramona.

"I made it home, Momma," Merena whispered as a tear rolled down her cheek.

A small noise caused Merena to jump in fright. Heart thumping, Merena turned around to see two young mermaids staring at each other in wonder. A large precious sapphire gemstone lay in the palms of their hands.

"We did it," one was saying.

An uncontrollable number of tears began streaming down Merena's face. She knew exactly who the mermaids were. A strong arm pulled Merena in tight. For an instant, Merena thought to fight, but then her body realized who it was.

"Jalen," Merena whispered as she looked up into her husband's handsome face. He was just as she remembered him. In fact, he didn't look like he had aged at all. His smooth dark complexion complimented his thick, dark, blue hair. Merena saw her reflection in his deep dark blue eyes. She must look twenty years older and completely deformed from all the scars. Those thoughts quickly disappeared as she got lost in her husband's eyes.

"I've missed you," Jalen whispered and then his eyes caught a glimpse of the twins, "Are they? How long was I gone? What exactly happened?"

Merena turned back around, "That's them. We've got a lot of catching up to do."

"Merena, your parents, I…" Jalen began.

A pain struck Merena as she touched the scars upon her skin, "I know… We will find a way through this. We will be fine. The Northern Sea Kingdom will thrive. It always does."

"Your brother. I never thought…" Jalen sighed.

Merena nodded towards the twins as she took her husband's hand, "They are all that matters right now, Jalen," Merena swam towards her daughters, "Hello." The bright crystal eyes of the twins looked directly towards Merena and Jalen.

"Mother! Father!" the twins exclaimed as they collapsed into the arms of their merparents. Merena let the fear, hate, and sorrows of the past years disintegrate as she embraced her daughters and husband. Her tears were no longer bitter but pure happiness. Merena wanted to say she was sorry. She wanted to take away all the pain that her daughters had experienced their entire life. But the words would not form.

"No magic in the world compares to this," one of the twins whispered.

Jalen squeezed even tighter.

Merena shook with great emotion as she whispered, "I love you, Jalen. I love you, Syrena. I love you, Nanami."

The twins glanced at each other at the sound of their real names. Their time as Evalyn and Adelia were over. It was time to start their new journey as the mermaids they were destined to become.

Magic flowed from the embracing royal merfamily. It sparked like lightning as it traveled throughout the Northern Sea Kingdom bringing light to every shadow. Stones rolled back into place and broken shells returned to their rightful beauty. The Northern Sea Kingdom was rebuilding itself. Mermaids and mermen embraced with joy. A band of dolphins tuned up their instruments, preparing to play. Crabs let out shouts claiming they were preparing a feast for everyone to enjoy. The magic swept through the ocean and to the other three kingdoms, healing any destruction in its path. Merfolk from all over began traveling to the Northern Sea Kingdom, following the trail left behind by the magic. As merfolk from the foreign kingdoms arrived in the Northern Sea Kingdom, everyone began to dance together in pure joy. There was no more fear in the sea. The Kingdoms were no longer divided, and the war had been won. The dark and unsteady waves that used to be hovered over by terrifying clouds up above vanished. The sun stretched its rays wider than it had in decades, warming the seas and lands. The balance that had been missing from the world had returned.

Epilogue

The sapphire stone that had been controlled by one person for thousands of generations now sat above the thrones of four leaders, the rightful royal family of the Northern Sea Kingdom. Its power was distributed between the blood of the four. A representation for all kingdoms of the sea of what happens when power is used for good and evil. Terror, destruction, and war was in the past. The four kingdoms were connected now more than ever before. Merfolk of all backgrounds lived in any kingdom they pleased. The waters above were once again safe for the merfolk to explore. Delight filled the waters above and beneath the waves, for the night skies were a mystical, ruby red. However, all must take warning if in the morning the sky continues to bleed that same red.

About the Author

Kiera Colson's passion is to spark purpose and joy in the people around her. She is a creator. Kiera always has a pencil in hand creating something new. At the time of publication, she is 16 years old and a rising high school junior. She is the eldest of four children. Kiera enjoys living a healthy lifestyle and actively learning new things for her future books. Connect with Kiera at www.kieracolson.com.

Connect with me!

Kiera Colson

SPEAKING ENGAGEMENTS
CLASSROOM PRESENTATIONS
EVENT APPEARANCES

kieracolson.com